Over and Under

The Underland Files
Book 1

Robin

*To Kat
Best wishes
Robin*

Copyright © 2023 by Robin Hart

All rights reserved.

No portion of this book may be reproduced in any form without written permission from the publisher or author, except as permitted by U.S./UK copyright law.

This novel is entirely a work of fiction. The names, characters and incidents portrayed in it are the work of the author's imagination. Any resemblance to actual persons, living or dead, events or localities is entirely coincidental.

Designations used by companies to distinguish their products are often claimed as trademarks. All brand names and product names used in this book and on its cover are trade names, service marks, trademarks and registered trademarks of their respective owners. The publishers and the book are not associated with any product or vendor mentioned in this book. None of the companies referenced within the book have endorsed the book.

Cover art by the awesome folks at MIBL Art www.miblart.com

Dedicated, as always, to my wife, without whom none of these books would ever see the light of day.

Note:
This novel is a re-working of "Underland: Warrior Stone Book 1",
undertaken with the permission and support of the original author, R B Harkess.

Contents

1.	One	1
2.	Two	12
3.	Three	19
4.	Four	29
5.	Five	39
6.	Six	48
7.	Seven	55
8.	Eight	63
9.	Nine	69
10.	Ten	75
11.	Eleven	83
12.	Twelve	90
13.	Thirteen	96
14.	Fourteen	102
15.	Fifteen	109

16.	Sixteen	119
17.	Seventeen	123
18.	Eighteen	130
19.	Nineteen	139
20.	Twenty	146
21.	Twenty-One	150
22.	Twenty-Two	158
23.	Twenty-Three	164
24.	Twenty-Four	169
25.	Twenty-Five	174
26.	Twenty-Six	185
27.	Twenty-Seven	191
28.	Twenty-Eight	198
29.	Twenty-Nine	206
30.	Thirty	212
31.	Thirty-One	216

One

My phone buzzed in my pocket, and I got a dirty look from the nerd sitting to my left when I didn't get to it fast enough. He had a point. Even though I switched it to silent before I sat down, it wasn't that quiet. Figuring it was a message, I took it out to check, but it was the timer telling me I had to leave. Now.

This trip was supposed to be for meeting friends and shopping in the mall at Hanlow, a twenty-minute bus ride from home. My mother was so relieved I said I had friends, she gave me a long pass for the day.

I didn't feel good I'd lied about it. Or about where I was going. I *had* taken a bus, but then I also took a train, and a ride on the Tube to get to a dingy cinema off Tottenham Court Road, in London. They were showing all three movies in the Space Odyssey set—you know them; the first one is 2001—on a 24-hour never-ending cycle. They started at midnight, and I figured I could get there in time for the second showing of the second film. Then I could watch all the films, just in the wrong order, and get home for 6PM.

And the phone was telling me I had just run out of time. If I wasn't home by curfew, there would be questions. Worse, they might check on my phone and see where I'd been.

Look, I know this makes me look bad. I'm not, but nobody was streaming them, I couldn't get hold of used copies on eBay, and I didn't have the money to buy them new. When I saw what the cinema was doing, it took me ages to screw up the nerve to do it.

I excused my way to the aisle, holding my bag up and out of the way, and headed up to the door at the back. As soon as I was through it, I loosened the strings on my hood and pulled it down. Having it up hadn't made me stand out in such a herd of nerds, but most of the audience were boys and I felt uncomfortable—so I pulled my hood up and hunkered down in my seat.

Outside, the London air should have stunk of car fumes, but after being in an oversize boy's locker room for so long, it was like walking out into a country meadow. I figured out which way I needed to turn, then jogged towards the tube station. Everybody said how manic they got during rush hour, and how the trains got so packed two or three might go by before you could push onto one. I was trying to slip through just before all that started.

People were crowding down the escalator, so I took the stairs. I was only halfway down when I heard the rails sing. The next train was already coming in, and who knew when the next one might be? A ten-minute delay could be a disaster. I leapt down the rest of the steps three at a time, then clung onto the handrail as I swung around the corner at the bottom. My head swum like I'd got up to quick and I staggered out onto the platform. The train was already there, and I heard the "pop-hiss" of the doors closing, so I launched myself through the nearest gap.

And tripped and fell to my knees, and my bag strap slid off my shoulder and down my arm. The doors clunked shut behind me and the train moaned away into the tunnel. I put my hand on the door to help myself up, then checked my knees to make sure I hadn't ripped my jeans (I hadn't). My cheeks were already burning, and I hated the thought of turning around to see everybody staring at me. But when I turned, there was nobody there. Not another soul in the carriage. I felt myself sigh, but it caught in my throat as I looked again.

Dim bulbs ran along either side of the ceiling instead of bright strip lights, and everything had a yellow tint to it. Leather loops rather than plastic-coated tubes hung down for people to hold, and the window frames were wooden, not metal. The floor was wooden too, with ridges filled with little plugs of something.

The train even sounded wrong, creaking and groaning as though everything was too much effort. It stank, not with the usual faint whiff of armpits and damp clothes, but with a stale smell of burnt tar. It took me a moment to figure out the little plugs in the floor were cigarette butts. That's why the train smelt so bad. People had been smoking. Inside. Disgusting.

The carriage wallowed from side to side and felt slow. I edged my way along it until I could see through the window of the connecting door, then rubbed my eyes. Didn't do any good. The next carriage was empty too and, when we hit a straight bit, it looked like I was the only person on the whole train. Which made no sense. Why would they run an empty train?

My eyes opened wide, and I grinned. Maybe it was some special engineering unit, like a test train, or a vintage train being used for a film shoot. Something 'period'. The grin faded when I realised I was in deep stinky for spoiling the shot, or trespassing. Whichever way I turned, it seemed I dug myself deeper into a hole.

The train slowed, and I hoped it was pulling into the next station. Maybe I could jump off and run away before anyone caught me. Or the old train would just creak away and I could catch a real one. Looking through the windows as the train burst out of the tunnel, I realised the station looked as wrong as the train. There were no bright lights, just lots of old bulbs that looked as though they weren't getting enough power. Everything looked the same smoky yellow.

A sign flashed past, and I was just able to read it. Fiddler's Green? There was no such station. Or maybe it didn't sound right? Unless it was the film set. I stepped back from the door and dropped onto a seat, waiting miserably for an irate director to yell "cut" as burly security people stormed in and threw me out of the station.

The brakes screeched so loud I put my fingers in my ears, then the train lurched to a halt. The doors hissed and opened like it was too much effort. Somebody in a long, dark coat leapt inside, through the same door I had stumbled through. The figure looked away from me, down the outside of the train and along the tunnel we had come from. It made me jump so much I squeaked like a Year 6. I hadn't seen anybody on the platform. The doors pop-hissed closed, and the figure turned.

It was a girl, I guessed two years older than me, dressed in a mad collection of clothes. The long coat looked like battered leather, or that weird waxy cotton some of my mother's 'country friends' wore. Beneath it, she wore a black top and camo trousers, with biker boots, or maybe Doc Martens. I glimpsed an army-style equipment belt festooned with little pockets and gadgets, and around her neck hung a pair of old flying goggles with blue-tinted lenses. In her right hand, she held a ray gun out of a Flash Gordon movie. Her dark hair frizzed like it dared anyone to come near it with straighteners. It all looked incredibly cool.

"Whoa," the girl said as she turned. "Who are you?"

"C-Claire." I wanted to kick myself for stammering, but this girl looked like some mash up from half my favourite stories.

"Evie. What are you doing here? It's not safe."

The train pulled away from the platform, then jerked and shook as though it had run over something. It kept moving, but the engine sounded even more unhappy. I grabbed a rail to stop myself from falling, but Evie just took a big step backwards.

"Come on," she called, and her heavy boots thudded on the wooden floor as she ran past me. I stared after her, confused. She reached the end of the car, pulling open the connecting door and looking back over her shoulder at me. "Hurry!"

I ran. There was an urgency in her voice that jabbed at my panic button. Both doors to the next carriage were open now, and the floor bucked and heaved on the other side of the gap. I could see the tracks ripping past beneath, and gory images popped into my mind of what would happen if I slipped.

"Take a big step," Evie yelled in my ear, her voice just carrying over the wind noise and the clattering of the wheels on the rails. "It's just like getting on an escalator." But I remembered all the signs I'd seen on the doors. 'Not to be used while train is moving. Danger of Death.' I can't help it. Mum is a stickler for following rules, and she has a voice that lives in my head.

Evie took the decision away from me. I felt a hand in the small of my back, then a shove at the exact right time to make me leap across the gap. Evie followed me a second later, pushing me away from the door then slamming it behind her and fiddling with the handle. I waited for the next thing to happen and she yelled at me, jerking her chin towards the other end of the carriage. "Go on. Get to the other end."

Without thinking too hard about why, I ran the rest of the way along the carriage and, half excited and half terrified I would get into trouble, opened the next pair of doors. Evie flashed me a grin as she ran past and jumped to the next carriage. Whatever it was we were doing, weird-girl seemed to enjoy it a little too much. Being honest, I had to admit I was, too. No doubt reality would bring everything to a crash stop in a minute or two, but while it was all unreal, why shouldn't I join in?

It only took us a couple of minutes to run the length of the train. Evie did something with the door handle again, then we were at the front of the train with nowhere to go.

"That should slow it down," she said.

"Slow what down?"

Evie threw a look full of questions at me, then glanced up and down my body. I flinched, but she didn't have the sneer the queen-bees wore when they did that to me at school.

"You aren't from around here, are you?"

I shook my head. "I'm not even sure where 'here' is." I looked back along the train, trying to see what we were running from, but we were on a curve that lasted for ever and I couldn't see more than one car behind us. The movie set idea seemed less likely every second. I was just opening my mouth to ask a bunch of stuff when Evie spoke first.

"Oh, no," she groaned. "You fell through, didn't you? By accident. Nobody recruited you?"

I shook my head. I was confused and getting uncomfortable, all of which made me snappy. "Look, what's—"

"Here is Underland," said Evie, pointing back along the train. "And that's a Morph. Well, that's what we call them." My eyes followed Evie's finger along the now-straight cars and saw a hulking shadow lurching towards us. I took a step backwards and took a gulp of air. It looked huge.

"Keep it together," said Evie. "You've done pretty good so far." She raised the gun and waggled it uncomfortably close to my face. "Besides, this'll take care of him, if we can get him out in the open."

I flicked my eyes from the wild child to the shadow and back again, not sure which was the biggest threat.

"So where is this 'Underland'?"

"The place between the Over and Beneath."

"Beneath what?"

Evie flicked me an impatient look and I almost bit back. "We live in the Over. The Morphs come from the Beneath. They want to find a way through Underland to get to the Over. We stop them."

"We?"

Evie looked over my shoulder. Her eyes narrowed and her lips tightened. I turned to see what she was looking at. The shape further down the train was growing larger. It looked wider than the aisle between the seats, and I was sure I could hear a ripping noise as it moved.

"Later," said Evie.

Evie turned to look out the window. Something bright flashed past, and she mouthed a count down from five as her hand reached up to the emergency signal. Was she kidding? We were in deep enough trouble. Pulling the emergency cord for a prank would dig us in so deep we would never get out, and I didn't want to add explaining a fine to the grief I was already going to collect from my parents for lying about where I was going.

But as I drew the breath to yell at Evie to stop, I figured the normal rules were suspended, or it seemed that way. If the hole we had dug for ourselves was the rabbit hole, we might as well go find Alice at the bottom. I reached out and grabbed hold of a pole just as Evie pulled hard on the bright red chain. The emergency brakes slammed on, and I watched the walls of the tunnel light up as sparks scattered from the screeching wheels. The train shuddered to a halt with only half the first car poking into the station. While it was still rocking on its springs, Evie threw the emergency exit lever over the doors and pulled them apart. "Move it," she called, and she leapt from the train.

I threw a glance back at the rapidly approaching hulk and jumped out after her, then followed her through an archway right in front of us. Through the arch was a hallway, where two wooden escalators—really. Wooden!—rumbled up and away to the right. More dim globes on poles between the stairs provided the light, and there was something odd about them. I know they weren't LED or anything like it, but they didn't look like old filament lights either.

Evie tried to push me onto the stairs moving up. I pushed back. Wooden escalators? I'd rather take the stairs. Except when I looked, there weren't any. Besides, Evie appeared to know what was going on, and I wasn't happy about walking away from that small reassurance.

"Go on," said Evie. "I'll be up as soon as I make sure it saw me."

"What?" I thought the whole idea was to get away from whatever was after us.

"I have to get it out into the open," Evie replied. "Then I can deal with it."

I stumbled as I stepped backwards on to the escalator and grabbed for the handrail. Evie flicked an impatient hand at me until I turned and jogged up the moving stairs. When I got to the top, I stepped to the side and turned back to watch.

Evie was side-stepping away from the bottom of the escalators, craning her neck to see as much of the platform as she could. Sounds of tearing metal echoed up from the platform, then a crash. She ran for the escalators as, too close behind her, a monster burst into the hallway.

The creature was about seven feet tall and blocky, with scaly skin that looked creamy-grey in the rubbish light. It stood on two legs, with muscly arms, and looked strong enough to rip a laptop in half the hard way. The head was like a crocodile, only the snout wasn't so long, and intelligent black eyes made it looked like a bad guy from an anime. The Morph—was that what Evie called it?—waddled, but it was fast and she could barely keep in front of it.

As she reached the bottom of the escalators, I watched Evie spin around and bring up the toy gun. It spat a fast-moving puff of something purple towards the Morph, missing its head by inches. Evie started up the stairs without waiting to see if she'd hit it. She only made it up ten steps, and the monster opened its mouth. I thought it was going to roar, but I could see right into its mouth. If that wasn't disgusting enough, there was a ball in there about the size of a baby's head. The tongue, with the lump on the end, leapt out like a frog's, and slapped Evie on the shoulder.

Except it didn't quite. Something stopped it dead, six inches away from Evie's back. The air underneath the ball sparkled like a vampire in daylight and Evie lurched forward, though it didn't look hard enough. I shook my head, for a moment thinking she was wearing some kind of personal force field. The situation was getting to me. She kept going, stumbling up the escalator, half on her feet and half on hands and knees. The Morph looked down at the red "Emergency Stop" button and swung a fist at it. The box disintegrated, glass shards and sparks scattering outwards as the monster hammered the metal frame flat. Both escalators rumbled to a stop. The Morph's maw stretched opened again. Before I could yell a warning, the tongue-fist-thing sprang forward and thumped Evie in the back. This time it connected for real and there was no sparkle in the air. Maybe I imagined it the first time? The fist landed so hard it made a sound like a drum.

Evie sprawled forward, arms flailing, ray gun flying through the air and landing on the other escalator. I winced in sympathy as she cracked her head on the edge of a step. Blood ran down into Evie's eyes as she turned herself over to face the Morph, climbing the stairs towards her. And I was standing there like an idiot. But what could I do? There wasn't even a fire extinguisher I could throw, and if I did, I might hit Evie.

"What can I do?" I yelled as the Morph loomed over the crazy girl.

"Stay back," Evie yelled, as she shuffled backwards. "Stinking bag of rot, get off me. Get off me." Evie snarled, but I heard her fear. The Morph changed, blurring and bloating, becoming colourless and translucent. A pouch grew out from its stomach and sank downwards. Evie tried to fend it off, yelling and cursing and beating at it with her fists.

I heard bacon frying each time Evie hit the pouch, but as it sank lower, she had less room to move. Then the bulging sac sucked her arms inside the Morph.

Sick burned the back of my throat. I took a half-step forward to go help, then stepped back. There was still nothing I could do. I could hear a voice inside my head screaming at me to find help, but my feet wouldn't move. Who would believe me? Besides, it was like I had to watch, to be a witness. Then I was almost sick again as the Morph dropped onto Evie and ate her.

I heard myself scream "No!" as Evie floated up from the ground, still struggling and twisting, until she was hovering in the middle of the Morph. The monster looked up at me and I clamped my hand over her mouth. Maybe calling attention to myself was not the smartest idea right now. Luckily, for me anyway, the monster turned away as if I wasn't important. As it moved away, it started to absorb its own arms and legs, stretching out until it looked like a slug with a bulbous head.

I couldn't see Evie's face at first, but I could tell she was struggling less. My stomach heaved again as I realised she would drown in whatever gloop filled the creature. The horrible thing slid away. Evie struggled more and spun around inside the gloop. Black splotches covered her eyes and mouth, and for one horrible second, I thought that something had eaten her face away. A moment later, as the Morph passed close to a light, I got a better look and saw Evie had pulled her goggles over her eyes and had stuffed another gadget in her mouth.

As the thing slimed away, I expected some kind of noise, like gurgling or scales rasping. Apart from the ticking of hot metal, there was silence. The Morph eased across the hallway at the bottom of the escalators and out onto the platform.

And I was alone at the top of the stairs.

Two

I turned my back on the escalator. Blood pounded in my ears and every breath felt like I had to force myself to suck in the air. What happened didn't feel like a dream—it was in colour, for one thing—but it had just got too weird. Was I asleep on the train? It would make things so much easier if I was.

I pinched my arm, but all I got was a red mark and some pain. If this was a dream, it was a full three-D VR. And if I couldn't wake myself up, I might as well get the most out of it.

Two corridors led away from the top of the escalators, one on each side. Tiles covered the walls and looked ordinary enough, if a bit old. Then I saw another station name—Regent's Walk—written underneath some weird shapes and it got weird again. I couldn't tell if the writing was painted on, or was under the tile glaze. It looked new and old at the same time. Then I noticed there were no adverts on the walls. Not even the grey metal frames for them to go in.

There were always adverts; even in old movies or documentaries about tube stations in the war; the walls were always covered with them. Just when I was feeling more comfortable, the place took weirdness to the next level. Which was when it occurred to me it was too quiet. It was late afternoon, almost rush-hour. Where were all the people?

I picked a tunnel and ran.

It went straight for about thirty yards, then curved left. After ten more steps, it opened out into a ticket hall, and I skidded on the tiles when I tried to stop. There were no automatic ticket barriers, just a low metal railing with a gate. Pitted paint flaked off the brass rail. Along the top was dull brown apart from where the brush of hands kept it polished.

On the other side of the railing, two brass-shelved windows were mounted in the wall. Next to them was a door marked 'Private'. At least they looked fairly normal until I noticed that the three lines of writing above the 'Private' looked like alien script . Black shutters pulled down inside said 'Position Closed', with the same strange characters. The English words were smallest and lowest, and I thought that ought to tell me something, but I couldn't figure what. There was no ticket machine, either.

I let the movie set idea go, comfortably normal though it might be. Special effects like the Morph didn't happen in real time; they took hours of post-production on powerful computers. This had to be real, somehow. My hands shook and sick burned in my chest. I had to find help, but from where?

I jumped over the rail and ran over to the ticket windows, then hammered on the glass. "Help! Is there anybody there? Please?" I tried the same at the door, then pressed my ear against it when nobody came. Silence. I kicked the door, then looked around in case anybody saw me.

I turned away from the ticket office and saw daylight. Sort of. It looked yellow, not blue, but not the yellow of streetlights. I ran towards it, but a metal gate was pulled across the exit. As well as a heavy metal lock holding the gate shut, a thick chain looped around the two sides, with a brass padlock as big as my palm. Through the grille, I could see a flight of steps going up, turning away like a spiral. There was a tiny rumble like street noise but too quiet, so I screamed for help as loud as I could.

My voice echoed back at me, and my heart sank as I realised I was wasting my time. Nobody would hear me.

I looked around the hall again, hoping for a phone, or an intercom, or even a bell to ring, but there was nothing. I turned away and headed back to the top of the escalators. There had to be other exits I could try.

But it was the same in the other ticket hall, everything abandoned or locked. My heart had been pounding since the moment I jumped on the train, but now I felt something different. I could breathe, but the air had no life to it, and I still felt short of breath. My heart wasn't pounding, it was racing, and my chest was aching like someone had kicked me. I had to lean against the wall when my ears buzzed, and my knees got wobbly.

Blinking away something in my eyes that I would not allow to turn into anything else, I turned away from the exit and trudged back to the top of the escalators. Each step felt like I was balancing along a beam, and I was rubbish at sports. Maybe there was something on the platform. An emergency phone, or another way out at the other end.

I couldn't take the first step. What if the monster was lurking on the platform? It might chase me back up here, and I'd already seen there was nowhere to hide. But what else could I do? Sit here hoping someone came to see why the trains weren't running? And given the station felt like it had been abandoned for a while, it could be ages before that happened. My knees trembled even more as I forced myself to take the first step.

Halfway down the escalator I found the gun Evie carried. I stepped over it, then sat on the next step down. Evie obviously thought it could do some good against that monster, so maybe I should take it with me? I made sure the dangerous end was pointing away from me, then looked it over. Despite looking like something out of the old Flash Gordon films, it did something, so I assumed it could be dangerous to me too. The trigger was obvious and right next to it a small switch pointing to a little red 'f'. The other position pointed to a green 's'. Other than that, it still looked like a toy, about a foot long and a grapefruit heavy.

I flicked the switch from 'f' to 's', pointed it towards the foot of the escalator and pulled the trigger. Nothing happened, so it was either safe or a fake. I pushed it into my bag.

Pulling myself back to my feet by grabbing the handrail, I tiptoed down the rest of the escalator, ready to run even though I knew there was nowhere safe to go. My heart was still hammering, but there was none of the clenching pain, and my chest wasn't so tight now. I kept muttering, 'don't panic' over and over again, like I was praying, which felt odd as it's something I've never believed in.

But even if I found a way out, what then? I was still a dozen stations away from home, and I had been stuck here for at least a half-hour. What good would it do to be out on the street in a part of town I didn't know? I had the money for a cab, but only from the last station, and I didn't have a clue if there was a bus I could take to get back to Liverpool Street. Phoning for help would be just too humiliating.

Phone?

I stopped and thumped my forehead with the heel of my hand. Phone!

It was deep in my bag, and it took some frantic groping around until my hand closed around the familiar shape and pulled it out. I put my thumb on the button. Icons flickered into life and, finally, the signal strength indicator. It immediately turned red. Of course. No signal. That would have been too easy. I stuffed the phone back into my bag and stomped down a few more steps.

Two steps from the bottom, I saw a silvery sheen on the floor. Maybe there was a cleaner, after all, with a mop or a polisher.

But when I looked closer, I realised it was a trail of slime tracking out onto the platform. How gross was that? But it did show me where the thing—Morph?—had gone. I followed it across the hallway at the bottom of the escalators and out through the arch.

Maybe I should have been more careful and peeked out onto the platform instead of walking right out, but nothing jumped at me. At the other end was a "Way out" sign, so I hurried towards it, feeling like a weight had lifted off me. As I passed in front of the train, I slowed without meaning to and looked back. And stopped.

Where was the driver? There was no slime around the front of the train, so the Morph hadn't eaten him. And where had the driver been when we stopped the train? I looked through the door of the cab, which was jammed half open. In the middle of the controls was a box, broken open, with complicated things inside. Automatic? So maybe nobody knew how bad the situation was.

I sat on a wooden bench, right where I could look into the wreck of the cab. This might not be a dream, but it wasn't real either. One side of my mouth lifted. If this wasn't my world, maybe I didn't have to play by the usual rules and be quiet little Claire with her nose in the nerdy books. I always discovered the trap before the hero and figured out how to escape, too. In my imagination, it was me crawling through all the secret tunnels, and I knew I could do as good a job as most of my heroes. Perhaps this was my chance to prove it. Or I could sit and wait for a cavalry that may or may not come, and all the while Evie was drowning or being digested or turned into an egg farm.

I stepped back inside the first carriage. The trail of slime was about as wide as the aisle, so I hopped from side to side to keep my feet out of it. Turned out the Morph had ripped out all the connecting doors, so it only took me a few minutes to hop-scotch my way to the back of the train, most of which was crushed inwards like a giant hand crushing a soda can. Only half the bulbs still worked, and they were flickering, but I could see the last pair of doors had been rammed into the carriage and were leaning at a crazy angle against their opposite numbers. The trail of slime went through the doors and vanished into the dark.

I stood at the hole in the train's side and stared out into the dark. There was some light from the bulbs in the carriage, but not much, and a light many yards along the tunnel wall threw a faint pool of grey onto the tunnel wall. Other than that, there wasn't much to see. There was just enough light to ruin my night vision, but not enough to make out any details. I leaned against the door frame and sighed. Failed already. No surprise. What was it that cow of an art teacher put on my report? "Claire has grandiose ambitions, but rarely the talent or determination to see anything through".

I stepped away from the door. The safest thing would be to walk back to the ticket hall and sit next to one of the grilles until someone found me. If only I had a torch or something.

I stopped halfway up the carriage, growled at myself, and thumped my head again before plunging my hand into my bag again. The phone was easier to find this time. I ambled back towards the door as I slid my finger around the screen, trying to remember where the torch was. There was a shortcut, but for the life of me... and I found it. A wide beam of bright white light shone on the floor and, for a few seconds, I couldn't take my eyes off it. It looked so clean. Then I turned it to point out of the door.

Fixed to the wall was a narrow walkway coated with slime. The harsh light from the torch cast sharp shadows and I couldn't be sure if what I saw was a rope handrail or a bunch of cables hanging in loops from the wall. Whatever it was, there was nothing between me and the walkway, so nothing to stop me from falling to the tracks if I slipped.

I squinted at the gap, trying to figure if I could simply take a big step across, or if I had to jump. That was when I realised the torch would be running the battery flat, so I switched it off and pushed it into an outside pocket of my coat. If I was going to do this, I would need both hands. The torch had done an even worse number on my night vision, and somehow it made jumping easier. If I couldn't see what I was doing, how could I be afraid of it. Or that's what I told myself. Edging halfway back across the carriage, I took three quick steps and jumped.

Three

My hands scrabbled across the gritty wall, but I couldn't find anything to hold on to. The slime was like slick ice, and my feet slipped every way, getting worse each time I tried to stop them and catch my balance. Could I jump hard enough to get back to the train, or was I going to slide under the train and onto the electrified rails? I was setting myself up to jump when a finger hooked over something solid. There was a handrail.

I grabbed it just as my feet slid out from under me, and I hung on for grim death. Jumping back onto the train was impossible now. I squeezed my eyes tight and tried to force myself to calm down and breathe slowly.

When I could open them again, they had adjusted to the light, and I could see a string of dim bulbs stretching down the tunnel. They turned the slime trail into a twinkling stream. I kept my eyes on the wall, careful not to look back into the train. There were wooden poles on the outside of the ledge, or path, and they had cables strung between them too, but high up, level with the top of the train.

With my left hand on the handrail, I reached my right out to the nearest pole, and with two things to cling to, I could stand up. I tried a step. As soon as I shifted my weight even a little, my right foot slid forward and out. Everything spun around, but I managed to get both hands back on the handrail, and the world levelled out.

Walking wasn't going to work, but as I dug my trainers from side to side, trying to find some kind of friction and looking in horror at the goop sloshing over my almost new Hi Tops, this insane idea came to me. I half-crouched, turned sideways to the direction I wanted to go, and shuffled my feet so one was in front of the other. With one hand holding the rail and the other on a pole, I pulled and slid forward on the slime. It was like riding a skateboard, only easier. I tried not to think of the goo sliding up over the toes of my sneakers and scooted myself along again when the next pole came in reach. It was fun, and I admit I giggled as I went faster and faster.

Until I lost my balance and slid towards the side of the ledge. Giggle turned into shriek, and I got serious, very quick. With my left hand on the rail, I eased myself back to the centre of the ledge, then set myself up again. I slid along until I saw a gap coming up in the walkway. Shifting my weight and holding the rail a little tighter slowed me down, and I stopped just before a set of steps. They dropped the ledge down to floor level, where there was a door. It was the same dark and dusty brown as the tunnel wall, and it was open.

The steps in front of me were coated with slime and looked deadly. Even with both hands on the rail, I had visions of slipping and cracking my back or my head on the edge of a step. But I had to get down them or turn and make my way back. The only way to get down safely was on my butt, and I very reluctantly sat and slid down each step. I almost threw up again as I felt the clammy slime seeping through my jeans. At least it was cold. I don't think I could have done it if it was warm. And reminding myself that a real adventurer wouldn't be so squeamish didn't seem to help.

There were no lights beyond the door, and no light switch I could find, so I scrubbed my hands on the wall, then on my jeans, getting the worst of the muck off before I dug the phone out of my coat and switched on the torch again. The battery was down to 40%, and I hoped it would last.

I scuffed my trainers in the dust to scrub off the worst of the muck off the soles, then I followed the trail into the corridor behind the door, hopping from side to side again, trying to stay on clean ground. The air was acrid with a tang of hot metal, and there were many doors, with vents top and bottom, and signs with lightning bolts saying, 'Electrical Hazard'.

The corridor took a left turn and stretched off ahead of me, no doors or junctions scarring the walls within the range of my torch. I could still see the trail. It seemed to get fainter, so I kept following it. Either something would come up, or I would get a better idea, or I would hit a dead end.

When a dark shape humped up from the ground at the edge of the light, I froze. If it was the Morph, waiting for me, it knew exactly where I was. I covered the light with my hand, then realised it was a waste of time. I stood still, holding my breath and ready to run. Only I didn't know where to.

Nothing moved. I counted to thirty, then edged forward. I couldn't stand and wait. The battery on the phone would go, for one thing. The mound resolved into a pile of earth, and beside it was an opening in the wall. It was oval, rather than rectangular, and not as tall as a normal door. I crept up to it and peered around the edge.

The passage beyond looked melted through the ground, rather than dug out, and something transparent covered the walls. It was hard and smooth when I ran my fingers over it, and my lip curled as I wondered if it was dried slime. I wiped my fingers on my jeans before I remembered they were already grosser than the wall.

The torchlight reached 30 feet or so along the tunnel, but I couldn't shake the feeling there was something just out of range, something I couldn't quite see. Almost like there was another light. I turned off my torch, closed my eyes, and counted a hundred heartbeats. When I opened my eyes, the whole tunnel shone with a soft green glow, bright enough to walk along the passage. I tucked the phone into my bag and tiptoed along beside the slime trail.

The tunnel curved to the right and the slope downward was steep enough I wasn't looking forward to coming back up. And that made me worry how deep I was getting, and about all the earth piled over me with no obvious support. It helped that the soft green glow wasn't bright enough to make out many details, but when I looked up at the roof, the skin along my spine flinched.

The light slowly increased, as though the tunnel was opening out on to somewhere. I eased closer and saw the tunnel ended in an opening off one side. I poked my head around the edge of the hole.

Unless it was a very odd shape, I could see most of the cave. It looked about as long as a soccer pitch, although not so wide, and as tall as our sports hall. Wooden boxes scattered here and there, some broken open, some whole. Blobs of jelly, stuck to the walls, shone with a sickly green light, and there were puddles of bright ichor seeping from them like thick dribbles of fluorescent snot. The floor looked unnaturally smooth, but there were stray rocks and boulders littered about.

At the far end, at the very edge of what I could make out, was the blobby shape of the Morph, or if not the Morph, then a Morph. Next to it was another, smaller blob that seemed to float in the air. It had a dark centre that made it look like a frog's egg, and I shuddered as I wondered if the thing was trying to reproduce.

I squinted and looked again. The dark centre in the egg, if that's what it was, seemed about Evie's size. The image of a fly wrapped up in spider silk popped into my head. If this went wrong, I could end up in a sack next to Evie. Would it keep me for food? Or worse? What if these Morphs injected their eggs into unwilling donors, like wasps? I pulled back as I dry-heaved, and my hands trembled.

For a moment, the thought of looking for other exits from the top of the escalators again seemed like a much better idea than hanging around here, but the thought of going back out into the dark and slippery corridors with a torch that was about to run out seemed almost as dangerous as trying to rescue Evie.

Creeping into the cave, I dropped to my knees behind a crate and took Evie's gun out of my bag. It still felt like a toy in my hand, and I put my bag on the floor before easing up to the side of the box. Grabbing the gun, I lifted it and sighted along the barrel, aiming towards the Morph. It didn't feel right. The gun was too short to hold like a rifle, and there were no little ridges at the back or front to line the shot up. And the Morph was too far away. Even though I had a clear shot, the thing was so close to Evie that I might hit her if I made a mistake. I had to rearrange things.

My throat was so tight I couldn't swallow, and my hands could only just keep hold of the gun. I would have to get closer to the Morph or get it to come closer to me. I dragged in three deep breaths, then stepped out from behind the crate.

"Hey! Over here. Come get me, blobby." I winced in horror as the last word left my mouth. Not cool. The thing flinched, then started towards me, transforming into the Manga monster as it moved. I had forgotten it could do that and I let out a scream. But I brought up the gun, and I pulled the trigger.

Nothing happened. I pulled it again and still nothing. The Morph had already covered thirty yards before I remembered

I put the safety on, then I wasted more precious seconds as I fumbled for the switch. I flicked it up with my thumb and levelled the gun at the Morph. The monster was only fifty feet from me now, its mouth gaping and something squirming inside. I aimed—sort of—and fired.

A tight cloud of purple shot out the front of the gun, missing the monster by a foot. The weapon kicked back so hard it knocked me off my feet, and knocked the gun out of my hand as I slid along the floor. The monster's tongue frogged out and passed so close over my face I saw the heavy mass at the end. It looked like a clenched fist dipped in slime, and I felt a breath of air as it passed.

When I stopped sliding, the gun was just out of reach. The Morph was almost on top of me now, snarling. I glanced up and saw a mouthful of pointed teeth. Its tongue was back in its mouth, but the mouth was still open, and something squirmed inside. I waited a second longer, then rolled right, towards the gun. The end of the tongue slapped onto the floor next to me with a noise like a raw egg breaking, then pulled back with a sticky rip. My hand scrabbled for the gun and swung it around to where I hoped the now-howling Morph would be. Hoped, but I wasn't sure. There was no way I could dodge its tongue again, and I didn't want to see it, or the mouthful of teeth, as they came down to end me, so I squeezed my eyes tight shut.

My elbow hammered into the floor and the gun ripped out of my hand again. Did I pull the trigger? Or had the Morph slapped the gun away? The snarl cut off with a pop and a waterfall of warm goo soaked me.

I wiped the slime from my face and tried very hard not to be sick. The goo was sticky and smelled of mothballs and dog food. I sat up, looked down at my clothes, and scowled. It was everywhere. Luckily, my mouth had been closed, but something was burning inside my nose and I did something disgusting I had only ever seen rugby players do, once for each nostril. The burning eased, but the smell didn't go away. My hair felt like I'd gelled it too much.

Once I slid to the edge of the pool, I rolled over onto my hands and knees, then found something to steady myself against as I stood up. Goo oozed down my legs, getting into and under my sneakers. It made walking so hard I almost got down on my hands and knees again, but there was no way I was crawling up to Evie like a baby. I shuffled up to the other end of the room.

Evie struggled inside the sac, but all she could do was spin in place. As she tried to reach the side, she rolled around to the centre again. The sac changed shape and seemed to make Evie's rolling worse. I touched it and snatched my hand away. It was warm, perhaps even warmer than a body, and felt alive. I clawed at the membrane with my fingers, even though every touch made my skin crawl.

It was too tough for my nails, which I keep short anyway. I tried to pinch it and tear it, but the slime over my hands made it slip through my fingers. The lack of progress made me mad. I'd done the hard bit, so why was this causing me such a problem? Slapping it didn't help, and only made it swing back and forth like a giant punch bag.

I glared at it, and it took a moment to realise Evie was waving her arms at me, which made her bob up and down in the gloop. Once she saw I was looking at her, she pointed to the floor, then made a stabbing gesture. I looked where she pointed. The stones were all rounded pebbles, but there was a broken crate. I stomped on it until it broke some more, and I could tear off a length of wood with a sharp end.

I turned and stabbed the sack. It bent inwards but wouldn't burst. A slow shove was no better. I was about to give up when I remembered you get most splinters when you're trying to be careful. So I tried scraping the rough end of the wood over the skin. On the second try, a sharp point of the wood caught on a wrinkle and the pod popped like a balloon. Gallons of disgusting gel spattered onto the floor and soaked my legs and sneakers all over again.

Evie sat in the puddle, wiping the worst of the mess from her face before pushing up her goggles and taking something out of her mouth. She looked up at me for a moment and burst out laughing. I glared at her for a moment, trying not to join in, but I couldn't help myself and started laughing too. All the tension and fear had burst with the pod, and now we were either going to laugh or cry. Laughing seemed the more heroic option. We slid to the edge of the new pool, me on foot and Evie sliding along on her backside, and at the edge I held out a hand to help Evie up.

"Thanks," said Evie, grinning. "Good save." She walked down the cave, scraping goo from her arms.

I stared at her back, and I knew my mouth hung open. Was that it? The ghoulish light made it impossible to see if Evie looked pale, and I could hardly demand that Evie hold out her hands so I could see if they were shaking. But if Evie wanted to play the cool game, I could too. I took a few quick, careful steps to catch up and joined her. "Sorry about the mess."

Evie walked over to the gun and picked it up. When she looked back at me, her face had lost its bravado and was deadly serious. "You did a brave thing coming down here."

I felt my throat tighten. The whole situation was suddenly a bit too much to cope with, but people my age never said things like that to me. I didn't know how to process it. "I didn't know how else to get home."

"Doesn't matter. You came," said Evie. They had reached the entrance to the cave, and I picked up my bag. When I looked up, Evie was giving me an odd look. "You'd be a hell of a good Warrior, you know. Can't believe nobody recruited you." I wanted to ask, "recruited for what?" but it seemed the world was going back to normal, which meant my tongue stuck to the roof of my mouth, stealing my words. Cringing inside, I used the state of my clothes to change the conversation to something safer. "I look a mess. What will my mum say?"

Evie laughed again. "Don't worry, this will all disappear when you go back to the Over."

"You mean this is a dream?" An icy block of disappointment appeared in my gut.

"Oh no," said Evie. A tight, animal grin curled her lips and her eyes seemed to shine. "This is as real as our world and twice as nasty. Any damage is permanent, and the cuts and bruises are still going to hurt. You haven't seen the tiniest slice of Underland. I meant what I said, you would make a great Warrior."

A thrill of excitement tingled through me, but the fear of opening myself up to another person squashed it. One careless, honest comment had cost me years of being shunned. I treasured Evie's words, but I couldn't trust that they weren't just for the moment. I settled for a noncommittal shrug. Evie looked surprised, then disappointed. "Never mind. You'll forget all about it in a few weeks."

"Doubt it."

"You will. That's the way it works. Memories of this place are... slippery."

I let out a half-hearted chuckle. "Isn't everything?"

Evie grinned. "Good point. If you don't keep coming here, though, it fades from your mind. Might be best for you in the long run. How did you get here?"

I explained about the unauthorised outing, and how I had almost missed the train and got dizzy and fell through the doors, all the time trying hard not to get too embarrassed as Evie's grin got wider and wider.

"Awesome," she said when I had finished. "Not the movies. Don't see the point in old science fiction. I meant the entire trip thing. You've got guts. So, do you want to go back to the station you started from, or home? At the station, I can drop you the instant you left, or if you want me to drop you at home, you'll get there now."

It didn't make a lot of sense to me, but I wanted to get in, keep the argument with my folks as short as possible, and sink into a hot, bubbly bath as quickly as I could.

"Home, please."

Four

I enjoyed maths at school, or didn't mind it. It was better than History. And Biology. Everything was better than Biology. But today I felt like I had grown an extra head.

Being ignored was my comfort zone. The influencers and fashionista blanked me because I wasn't stick thin and didn't wear designer everything. By definition, I could never be their version of cool, and when they tried to bully me, they found out how much I didn't give a whatever about them. They didn't know what to do with that, so they decided I didn't exist. Which worked fine for me. Likewise, the jocks, although to be fair, most of them were serious about their sport and didn't mess around too much.

Then there were the geeks and nerds, all in their different tribes: chess club, band, and the computer club that never played any games. And there was the group mad for fantasy stuff, like magic and vampires and shifters. That should have been where I fitted right in. They should have been my people. It wasn't a big group, two or three girls from each year, but it still made no sense that every one of them should stop talking to me simply because I disagreed *once* with the boss bitch, and about something I couldn't remember any more. I tried apologising, but it was like I had the plague. Still, it was what it was.

That left the Goths and Amos and the Dweebs. Whilst I would never intentionally be mean to a Dweeb, I had nothing in common with them, and the Emos were too self-obsessed and depressing. That left the Goths, and I didn't have the nerve. I loved the look and the music, but they scared the stuffing out of me. My mum would have a litter of kittens if I brought one home.

So I wandered through school on speaking terms with most, but with no real friends. Largely ignored, which suited me fine. Until I went to that stupid cinema. I never had the nerve to brag about it, because there was nobody to speak to. Without someone to share the confidence with, there was no way to get my heroic act circulated without doing it myself, and that said "look at me" so loud it was desperate. All I got out of it was a pointless month-long grounding. I never went out anywhere, but mum decided they should take a stand, and dad was "being supportive".

But the one thing that had changed was fantasy geeks. It seemed every time I turned around, at least one of them was watching me. If there were two, then they covered their mouths or hid their faces, and I just knew they were talking about me. It had started off as being sort of amusing, but now it they just annoyed me.

Melanie Styke, the very queen bitch I fell out with, was the worst of them. She was older than me, in Year 11. Whenever I caught Styke watching me, she was scowling, like I'd offended her again. It was disturbing and aggressive and I hadn't a clue why.

So lessons with too many geek squad members in them were no longer fun, and neither was lunch. It seemed that wherever I tried to hide, someone would find me, and I spend the break trying to ignore sneaky glares and stares as they tried to make it look like they weren't watching me.

Today, the Maths class finished morning school. I stuffed my books into my bag and hurried to my locker. Lunch and my iPad swapped places with my schoolbooks, and I slipped out of the main building and into the grounds. I wouldn't embarrass myself by breaking into a run, but I walked quick. The best places filled up quickly. The prime locations were always dominated by one group or another, depending on how secluded they were and what the group was intending to get up to, but I was happy to find somewhere quiet. I only wanted to read and munch in relative tranquillity, and you could waste the whole break looking for the right spot if you were picky.

There was an empty bench around the corner from the doors to the toilets. My nose twitched, but the bench was on the girls' side, so it probably wouldn't smell too bad. I planted myself in the corner, put my back against the wall and stretched my legs out along the bench. My earbuds plugged into the iPad, and I tried to immerse myself in my book so I could ignore the two girls from Year 8 that sat under a tree only ten yards away from me.

The quality of the light falling on the iPad changed and made the screen look bright. It wasn't quite a shadow, but somebody was standing next to me. I scowled and ignored whoever it was, hoping they would take the hint and go away, but the sense of presence remained. I paused the music, twitched a bud out of one ear and looked up to deal with the intrusion.

It was a girl. She had a cocky grin on her face, but she looked out of place. A moment later, I realised the girl didn't belong here. She was wearing a uniform of sorts - grey jumper over a white shirt, a grey skirt that was way too short, and thick black tights – but the lack of a tie and the heavy boots would both have got her sent home and earned her a deferred detention. Still, there was something about her that looked familiar. Perhaps it was the wiry hair. But who would break *into* a school?

Whoever she was, the girl seemed to know her.

"Shift the legs, Claire. Lemme sit down. We need to talk."

Interesting. Claire, not Stone. Not sure why, I drew up my knees to make space at the end of the bench and popped the other bud out of my ear. It seemed typical, and deliciously ironic, that the only kid in the school who wanted to talk to me wasn't even supposed to be there. I tried to get my right eyebrow to go up on its own. I practised in the mirror, and it worked about one time in six. The other five I looked like an idiot so I settled for raising both. "We do?"

The older girl gave me a hard look as though she was searching for something, then she saddened as though she hadn't found it. "Damned memory leak," she muttered.

That impressed me. Most people couldn't get away with saying something like that and still look serious.

"I need you to think really hard, Claire," said the girl, looking straight into my eyes in an uncomfortably intense way. "About six weeks ago, you went into London. To a movie."

I nodded, eyes narrowed. This wasn't common knowledge, but it wasn't a secret either. "Three, actually. So?"

"What happened when you left?"

"I went home. And caught a pile of trouble."

"In more detail."

"Why?"

"Humour me."

My forehead crinkled. I wanted to move back from this child of weirdness, or at least look away, but there was something in her eyes. They were grey, with a black band around the outside, and I wished I had cool eyes like that.

"Focus," she said, almost snapping at me. "What happened when you left the pictures?"

"I went to the underground station and caught the train."

"Is that all?"

It seemed really important to whoever this person was, so I concentrated and tried to play the night back in my head. I remembered that the time seemed to fly by, that the movies were great, even if I felt a little uncomfortable being one of the very few girls there. "Pretty much. My phone buzzed. I left. I had had to run down the stairs to catch my train." But there was something else, something hiding just out of my memory's eye. I felt my frown dig in deeper and saw the look of disappointment on the weird girl's face get more intense. There was a hint of desperation there, too.

"What was the next station the train stopped at, Claire?"

A name popped into my head, and I almost said it out loud before I remembered there was no such station. I tried again, but the name stuck. "Fiddler's...Green?"

The older girl's face lit up, mouth twisting into a lopsided smile. I pushed a finger into each temple and rubbed, like I was popping a mental zit. My memory spat out an image of the girl in front of me, but wearing a weird pair of goggles around her neck and -

"Evie?"

"Yes!" the older girl hissed, grin turning savage for a moment as she made a tight punch with her right fist, then the expression collapsed into one of relief. "Shit, you had me going there. I was worrying you were too far gone."

I was about to ask what she was talking about, then I remembered our last conversation. "Oh, the memory fading thing, right?" Then my mouth dropped open, and my eyes strained wide as everything else flooded back, drowning my mind and spilling through my memory in a foam. My whole body shook.

Evie must have slid off the bench and knelt next to me; I felt her hand on my shoulder, squeezing gently, and it anchored me to a reality I felt was slipping through my fingers. "Hold on. It only lasts about a minute. You'll be OK."

Images flashed and flickered in my eyes, and smells tingled in my nose. I took my hands away from my face, stared at them for a moment, then put them on my knees and let my breath out with a whoosh. "How could I have forgotten?"

Evie gave my shoulder a last squeeze and moved back to the bench. "That's the way Underland works."

I swung right to put my feet on the floor and noticed that there was only one geek squad spy watching me now. Even from a distance, she looked agitated, which made me feel uncomfortable. It took me a moment to realise Evie was talking again.

"... a Warrior."

"I'm sorry?"

"I know. Amazing, isn't it? I had to argue with the council for hours until they agreed, but I beat them down. The job is yours if you want it."

I groaned inside. Evie looked pleased, proud and excited, all in one, and had obviously told me something she thought was impressive. Now I either had to make her rewind and start again, which would look rude, or go along with it (dangerous), or act like I didn't care. Rescue came in the unlikely form of Melanie Styke, striding around the corner with another Year 10 girl in tow. She was, as usual, turned out in a full skirt and blazer, with her prefect pin perfectly placed on her left lapel.

"I don't know who you think you are, but you are not supposed to be on these grounds and unless you leave this school, I'll report this... to... a..."

The finger Styke had been waving in front of Evie slowed and stopped as she caught up with what her lieutenant was whispering into her ear. She sniffed, frowned, then backed away a step. The two Year 8s hovered a few feet away; far enough out to keep out of trouble, close enough to hear every word. "Yes, whatever." Her bluster level picked up again. "You are still not supposed to *glerk*."

Evie rose to her feet and took four quick steps to put herself right in Styke's face. The prefect tried to back away, but Evie was too quick. She grabbed Styke's lapels in her fists, turned, and shoved the prefect against the wall.

"Do *not* speak to me like that," said Evie. She hadn't hit Styke with the wall that hard, just enough to make a point. But her voice was dead and level.

"Wha?" Styke still tried to argue. "But--? You can't—"

"Do this?" Evie pulled her back and hit her with the wall again. "I can and I will because I'll bet that you are supposed to be the Recruiter here, eh? What was your name? Shite, or something?"

"St-st-styke."

"That's right. I looked it up before I came."

"Who-?"

"Start with *why*?" Evie suggested, giving the lapels another shake.

"Why?" Styke agreed.

"Because I want to know how you could have been so damned stupid as to have missed one of the best prospects I've seen in years."

"What, her?" Even pinned against the wall, Styke still managed to slap me in the face with her words.

Evie cocked her head to one side. "Surely you aren't referring to the drop-through who only three weeks ago managed to track a Morph and rescue a Warrior? Don't tell me you are so far out of the loop that nobody told you that story?"

"Look, she isn't one of *us*," Styke said, an edge of desperation in her voice. "I knew she'd been down. We could smell it on her. So we followed standard procedure and watched her."

"Standard procedure is that you refer any candidates to the SFU for approval and possible contact."

"Yes, well, she's too old now anyway," Styke shot back, sounding more confident and trying to prise Evie's hands off her lapel. Evie gave no ground.

"Really? You need to jump in occasionally and pick up on the news, because if she's not one of *us*," Evie drew the word out sarcastically, "then how come she is being offered a provisional direct entry as a Warrior?"

Styke froze, and there was a collective gasp. "They can't do that," Styke hissed, and I didn't miss the hateful, jealous glare Styke shot at me.

"I talk fast," said Evie, smiling in an entirely humourless way, "and I bullied them into it."

Styke's body sagged as she gave in to the inevitable. "Who are you?"

Evie grinned, letting go of Styke's lapels and giving them a gentle tug to settle them back into place. She fiddled with the Prefect pin, making sure she lined it up perfectly, then put her face uncomfortably close to Melanie's. "The name," she paused, "is Jones."

A susurration of whispers broke out around Styke's little band of helpers, and they took a collective step back. Melanie swallowed so hard Claire could see her throat working.

"*Evelyn* Jones? Warrior Evelyn Jones?"

Evie nodded, grinned with the same warmth as a tiger, and Styke's face went very pale. Evie gave her blazer one more pat, then sat down next to me again.

"That's right, so if you people wouldn't mind, I have a job to offer here and I would rather do it in private." Most of the group disappeared before Evie had finished speaking. Only Styke seemed intent on dragging her heels, but even she eventually turned and walked away. Evie waited until she was about to turn the corner at the end of the wall before she called out to her. "And Shite—"

"That's 'Styke'."

"Whatever. No teacher running around the corner in five minutes, and no messing with Claire. You understand me? Fully?"

There was a hint of rebellion in Styke's eyes, but it faded, and she nodded once before walking away. Evie leaned back against the wall and chuckled. "That was fun." She looked over at me and her face fell into a defensive semi-pout. "Come on, Claire. The bitch should have picked you out years ago or reported you to whoever had the job before her. Let me guess. You don't get on? Something personal?"

I nodded and Evie looked smug. "Thought so. I can spot her type every time. Still, maybe you won't have to worry about her anymore, eh?"

I cocked my head to one side, realised I had done it, and put it straight. "Why?" Then I realised Evie was talking about whatever it was I hadn't heard before Styke interrupted. "I'm sorry. I think I missed something."

"Keep up," said Evie, shaking her head. She stopped and stared at me. "How would you like to be a Warrior?"

My mouth opened, but my brain had nothing to pass on. The whole idea was ridiculous, unexpected, impossible. Wasn't it? I realised I was staring at my hands again and raised my eyes to look at Evie. She looked disappointed, even embarrassed, like a friend who'd given you an awkward birthday present. The bell chose that moment to ring. "I have to go," I said, standing, then looking down and feeling relieved that I didn't have to answer right then.

"Is that a 'no'?" Evie asked.

"Not no, but..." I took a deep breath. "It's unexpected. I only just got my memory back. This on top is overload."

Evie nodded. "I understand. They said I could be your instructor. If you want. They wouldn't throw you out on the street."

"I have to go."

"Can we talk again? Today?"

I edged away. I wanted to pass on the offer. Most of what I remembered was scary and dangerous. Still, a part of me needed to know more. And Evie was looking at me like a puppy that had been told off and I didn't have the heart to just send her away.

"Remember where I live?"

Evie nodded.

"This evening, seven o'clock. Wait at the gate, out of sight. I'll make up an excuse to come out."

She probably nodded, or something, but I was already turning away. I had to run to my locker, and I was going to be late for History.

Five

The rest of the day was a disaster. There was a major increase in background muttering and pointing from the geek squad, which had spilled over so that some of the other cliques were staring at me too. I felt like the only one wearing fancy dress at a party, and concentration wasn't an option. Plus, my memory seemed determined to keep playing that absurd night over and over, like it couldn't quite believe it had happened, or was embarrassed it had forgotten it. No matter how hard I tried to focus, my thoughts wandered about like a butterfly. I even got "words" from two teachers before the afternoon was over.

Things were no better when I got home. Mum, in an act of superhuman self-sacrifice, had cooked me microwaved sausages with mashed potatoes and baked beans. I smiled, thanked my devoutly vegetarian mother for polluting her vinyl-gloved fingers with processed dead animal flesh, and tried very hard to eat. Joking aside, it was a thing for her to do that for me. But my appetite was as messed up as my concentration. I made a point of eating all the sausages, though.

Seven o'clock took forever to arrive. We had a family thing that we all sat around in the lounge for an hour after dinner. As usual, the news was on, but I felt like I was non-stop fidgeting.

With ten minutes to go, I still hadn't thought of a decent excuse for going out, so I kept it simple.

"I feel all antsy," I got up from the couch, next to my dad. "I'm going to go for a walk."

"Good idea, sweetie." Mum was enthusiastic about everything she didn't disapprove of. "Blow the cobwebs out. I swear by it. Just be careful by the road."

I turned away, hiding my smile. Mum's head had been filled with cobwebs and dandelion fluff since I could remember. So far, there was no sign of it blowing away, and I loved her for it. Heart the size of an elephant, brain the size of a bat, and I had heard my dad mutter that to himself, so I didn't feel bad saying it too. I opened the front door and waved my hand outside. It wasn't cold enough for a coat, so I snibbed the latch and pulled the door shut behind me.

The sky was spring blue, dotted with candyfloss clouds edged with pink from the setting sun. My sneakers made a satisfying crunch on the gravel, and I sounded like a squad of soldiers marching in parade. A head poked around the hedge, but Evie pulled back too fast for me to wave at her. When I got to the gate, I looked back at the house to see if anyone was watching me. "Quick. Over here."

Evie darted around the corner, and we set off at a jog until the house disappeared behind the barn on the edge of the yard. Evie leaned against the wall. She had dropped the bogus school uniform and was wearing camo pants and a dark top with a deep "V" neck. I could see a pendant hanging around her neck, a complex pattern of wires coiling around a wooden frame, with a dark red stone in the middle. It looked home-made. I flicked a glance at Evie's face. She looked as edgy as I felt.

"Nice place," said Evie. "Farm?"

I shook my head. "Used to be. We converted it and sold off most of the land. We kept a couple of the smaller fields and rent them to people with horses. Dad says it's keeping a gap between us and the developers. My mum uses this for her 'craft shop'." I pointed at the barn, felt my eyes roll.

"Sounds cool," said Evie.

I knew she was only being polite and shook my head. "She's not very good. Other people make most of the stuff she sells, but it makes her happy, I guess."

An awkward silence fell. I couldn't look Evie in the face, and she fiddled with a splinter of wood sticking out the side of the barn. "So what did you want to talk about?"

"The offer, obviously." Evie snapped, and I took a half-step back. She pulled a sour face. "Sorry. I'm no good at this sort of thing. Remember I said you'd make a good warrior?" She waited for me to say something, so I nodded. "Well, after I brought you home that night, I got to thinking. We're short of warriors. I guessed you wouldn't want to start at the bottom, so I went to the council and argued with them. I got them to agree that you could come in as a sort of direct entry. If you wanted to."

I got as far as opening my mouth to trot out the speech I had ready. How I'd thought about it, and while it had been exciting in a way, it had also been really scary and dangerous, and I didn't think it was a good idea. But the words wouldn't come out. I looked up and saw Evie's face turning pink, and that look of disappointment coming back. I wondered what it cost her to arrange this deal, and how hard it was for her to come and ask me.

"Not sure," I said, falling back on the truth. "Do I have to say yes or no right now? There must be a million questions I should ask first, and I've only got a half hour before they wonder where I am."

Evie looked flustered for a few seconds, then her face lit up and she snapped her fingers. "I'm an idiot. How about I show you? Or start to, at least?"

"How?"

"Let me take you there. We can have a look around, and you can ask questions until your lips cramp."

"In thirty minutes?"

Evie's smile got even wider. "Your folks won't even know you've gone. Promise."

I looked right into Evie's face, trying not to let it show I thought she was crazy. Evie met my eyes, and I shrugged. "Alright."

Which was not what I had meant to say. I meant to make another excuse.

She stood so close beside me I could feel her body heat through my sleeve. Then she linked her arm through mine, latching on too tight and making me feel a little uncomfortable. "Once you get the hang of it, it'll be a lot easier. So all we do now is a quick walk forward. Ready?"

I wasn't sure I was, but I nodded anyway. Evie gave a count of three, and we stepped forward. On the second step, without warning, she pulled me hard to the left and spun me around. I felt a dizzying moment of vertigo, then I was stumbling as she fought to keep my feet under me.

"See. Easy," said Evie, keeping hold of my arm. "Just stand for a moment and get your balance back."

Her voice sounded wrong, echoing like we were inside, and I realised I still had my eyes screwed shut. I opened them and felt giddy all over again. We were in a large room with a checkerboard pattern of tiles on the floor and a matching pattern on the wall facing them. Evie, still holding on to my arm, gave a gentle tug.

"Are you OK? We need to get off the pad."

I took a deep breath, looked from side to side, and let the breath puff out again. "Guess so." She led me towards a door. "So where are we? Are we in this 'Underland'?"

Evie nodded. "Thought you might be able to tell. Doesn't the air taste different?"

I experimented with the idea, breathing through my mouth, then my nose. There was something metallic and smoky, but so slight I could have been imagining it. She shrugged.

"This is the SFU—" Evie started. I interrupted her straight away.

"SFU?"

"'Special Facilities Unit'," Evie explained. "It's who we work for down here."

"And what do we do?" I asked. When I didn't hear an answer, I looked up to see a half-smile tugging at the corner of Evie's mouth. I was going to ask what the joke was when I realised I'd said 'we', not 'you'. Now there was something to think about. "Slip of the tongue."

"Let's get you some basic kit first. Don't want to go out naked."

"Pardon?"

"Local slang. Sorry."

We walked along a corridor that looked much like any other corridor in an old building, but there was something not right about it and it took me several minutes and a flight of stairs to figure out what it was. "Are those gas lights?" I pointed at one of the sconces, where a ball of yellow-white light bobbled behind a shade of frosted glass.

"No, not gas," Evie said, another grin hovering around her lips. I let her hold on to her stupid secret and followed her to a double door. A sign pinned on the right-hand door said 'In: This Side ONLY'; handwritten in an elegant copperplate and neatly underlined several times. Evie pushed the other door open and stepped inside, her gait changing to an insolent swagger. I followed, using the right door.

The room was enormous, filled with shelves and racks that seemed to go back as far as I could see. Ten feet from the door was a counter that stretched the width of the room. Iron bars rose to the ceiling, with three serving hatches built in. Only one was open, and behind it stood something slightly shorter than me, with wrinkled grey skin and eyes like a goat. Its ears were tiny, and an arc of ridges and bumps ran around its eyes like spectacles. Its hands were surprisingly small, with only three very dexterous-looking fingers.

"Jones," it said. "Predictable as ever. Surprise me one day by coming in through the same door as everybody else." The voice was dry, and the consonants all seemed to have a click in them somewhere. I felt Evie nudge me with an elbow and realised I was staring. I pasted a smile onto my face and tried to look friendly.

"New?" said the thing behind the counter, jerking a pointy chin in my direction.

"How could you tell?" said Evie, tone sarcastic. "Probably a trainee."

"Probably?" Ridges moved on the creature's face, either side of its eyes, and I guessed it had done the equivalent of raising its eyebrows.

"Long story. You should have her in the books; look under Stone, C. I think her number is 2149."

"2146," the creature corrected. "Basic equipment?"

"And a Kevlar. And a locker."

"Size?"

I realised they were both looking at me, and my cheeks got hot. "What size?"

"Any size, so long as it's yours," said the creature behind the counter.

I admitted to being a 12. The door over the serving hatch slammed shut, and the creature walked away. I looked at Evie and raised my eyebrows, but Evie put a finger to her lips. So I was to wait. The creature returned in a few minutes carrying a cardboard box a two feet long and an foot wide. On the top was a clipboard with a form on it. The creature put the box on his side of the mesh, opened the door, and pushed the clipboard through. "Sign this."

I took the clipboard, studied the list of eight items, and handed it back. "No. Not until you hand over the box so I can check it against the list."

The silence that followed seemed to last minutes, and the store-thing's slit pupils bored into me like it was furious I'd argued with it. Then it barked a loud, "Ha", and slid the box through the hatch. I checked through the box, went down the list, signed, and handed the clipboard back.

"At least she has a brain," said the thing behind the counter, looking at Evie. Then it turned back to me and gave me the faintest of bows. "I am Krosset, storesmaster. You need anything else, you come to me. With a requisition. Your locker number is 23." It slammed the hatch door closed and walked off into the depths of the racking.

"That was odd," I said, stating the obvious, but feeling I had to say something.

"At least he liked you."

"He did?" And now I knew Krosset was a he.

"Of course." Evie pulled a wry face. "Sorry. I'm not making a good start as a teacher. Krosset is a Grenlik. It's really rude to ask a Grenlik for their name, and they only offer it if they don't think you're a waste of space. If you don't know it, or people you're with might not know it, just call them Grenlik."

I nodded, trying to take everything in. Evie led me down another corridor and into a room full of metal lockers. There were eight rows, each twenty lockers long, and there were long wooden benches set along the walls. My locker was at the end of the room, and the door was already open. Evie showed me how to set a new combination using a gadget on the back of the door that looked like an exploded clock. I shook my box at her.

"How much of this stuff do I need right now?"

Evie rummaged through the box, taking out the long coat, a pair of goggles, and something on a leather cord. "Just these for now." She looked at me with a critical expression. "Should have thought this through a bit more, I suppose. But I'm not on duty. We'll be OK."

I looked at Evie, then down at myself. I was wearing black yoga pants and ballet pumps with a baggy top. Evie wore grey camo pants and heavy boots. I put the box into the locker and slammed the door shut. Then I took the coat from Evie and tried it on. It was a good enough fit, but it felt heavy. When I looked up, she had the goggles dangling from one hand and a thin cord from the other. She shook the goggles at me and said, "Pocket". Once I'd done that, she held her fist out until I put my hand under it, then she dropped a pendant, just like the one I saw her wearing, into my palm. It looked less worn and the red ball in the middle was the bright red of fresh blood, rather than the dark wine-red of Evie's.

"What's this?" I turned it around and saw the number 2146 engraved on the back.

"Put it on, against your skin," said Evie. "It's the most important thing you own down here." I hung it around my neck as she walked away, dropping it under my top. Did I feel a faint tingle when it first touched me, or was I imagining things? I hurried after Evie, but as I turned into the same aisle she had gone down, something flew towards my face. I had no time to duck or catch, but whatever it was bounced away when it was still a foot from my nose. This time I was sure my skin tingled where the amulet touched it. Evie grinned at me from behind a locker door. The number on the locker, seventy-seven, stuck in my mind.

"The amulet is a Personal Protection Device. We call them Kevlars. Think of it as a kind of stab vest."

"Stab vest?" I said, then winced when I heard how shrill my voice sounded.

"Come on," said Evie. "Let's get out of here. I know a great café not far away. My treat."

I nodded. We left the locker room and followed a maze of passageways until we reached a more substantial looking door. Evie touched a brass plate, which glowed a warm yellow, and there was a loud click from the lock. Evie grabbed the handle and pulled.

The first thing I noticed was there weren't enough colours. Everything looked washed out. Not as bad as the monochrome orange of a streetlight, but close. I looked up at the sky. It was an insipid yellowish, off-white that had no texture. The next thing I noticed was the mountain I was fairly sure shouldn't be there.

"W...w...?" I gave up and pointed.

"Hyde Mountain," said Evie, her mouth twitching as she tried not to laugh. You think that's freaky, look behind you."

I turned, stumbled, and gasped. "But that's the Tower of London. We were just in the Tower of London? What's it doing here?"

"Mostly the Tower," Evie agreed. "But look again."

I did. "It's different. It's too big, and some of those buildings shouldn't be there."

"And that's Underland in a nutshell," said Evie, jerking her thumb along the path to show they should get moving. "It's just enough like home to let you think you know where you are and what you are doing, then it trips you up and you land flat on your face. It's not London. Remember that."

Six

We walked through a checkpoint and out onto the street. The road wasn't as busy as I would have expected in *my* London, but foot and road traffic were busy. Only it wasn't people on the pavement, and the traffic wasn't cars or trucks. The pedestrians looked like movie extras and some of the cars looked right out of old silent movies. The larger stuff all seemed to be carriages and carts—but without a horse. Instead, they had things that looked like miniature steam engines, but running on rubber wheels and with no chimney. I forced myself to turn away, because I was gawping like a tourist, and I knew it wasn't a good look. I hoped Evie was going to start with the explanations soon.

The buildings looked old, but no more than I expected, and I caught sight of a road sign that said we were on Great Tower Street. The foot traffic melted out of our way, but I didn't miss the sideways glances, suspicious and distrustful. Evie dragged me onto a quieter road, and halfway down we went into a café. There were some tables set up in the street, sheltered under white umbrellas.

Evie gestured I should take a seat at a table away from the road, then tapped politely on the window before plonking herself in the seat opposite me. The door opened a minute later, and Evie kicked my ankle. I was gawping again. The being standing in front of us was easily seven feet tall and looked somehow rectangular, like the Easter Island statues. She wore a pale blue smock, sleeveless and ankle length, belted at the waist with a thin cord. On her feet were sandals, held in place by thongs. The notepad she held to take our order was school size but looked small in her hands.

"Good day, Warriors. How may I help you?

"Good day, Sa," Evie replied. "A pitcher of squash and two glasses, if you would?"

"It will be my pleasure. Chilled?"

Evie smiled and nodded. The waitress gave a stiff bow from the waist before turning and walking back into the shop.

"You've really got to stop that," said Evie.

I was about to ask what when I admitted I already knew. "Sorry. It's all so—unexpected."

"Get a grip. Underland isn't safe, Claire. It's not a theme park. That's why you have the Kevlar. We're still kids, but we do a very grown-up job here."

"Start there, then. What does this place need us for, and why not adults?"

"Because as you get older, it gets more difficult to get through. I've got another two years, maybe three. My snapback will get shorter first, and then I won't be able to get in at all. Three months after that, I won't even remember I was here, and I wouldn't believe it if I wrote it down." I saw sadness pull at the corners of her eyes and must have let it show on my face. Evie made a brushing-away gesture with her hands.

"Will you forget it? For real?"

Evie's face looked haunted. "I'd bloody well better, because I am terrified that a part of me deep inside will remember this place, and somehow I'll still miss it."

"You like it that much?"

Evie nodded, then made an obvious change back to the original subject. "They need us because humans are the best there are at detecting Morphs as they break through, and then tracking them down and stopping them. And we have a certain amount of protection."

"I thought you said it was dangerous," I said, then sat back when Evie glared at the interruption.

"We recruit kids with weirder imaginations, about Year 7. Oddly, more girls than boys. Not too many. Not even from every school. They get some training and acclimatisation topside, then they come down here. They get more training and work as runners. If they last, they make Observer. There are Observer stations all over the place, every city, every region. If they get a sighting, a breakthrough, a runner gets sent to a Warrior, if there isn't one at the Obs Post. The Warrior goes to the incursion site, tracks the Morph until she can burst it."

I could hear the 'W' on Warrior, now, but the idea made me pull a face. "That sounds so gross. Can't we just send them back?"

"The alternative is worse. We don't know how they do it, but if we don't get them here, then a Morph can ascend and get to the Over." She put up a hand as I tried to interrupt again. "No, not as a monster. They change, become something like a virus or a ghost. They infect people and change them."

I started to laugh but choked it off when I saw naked fury in Evie's eyes. "No joke, Claire. Nobody knows why they do it, but the hosts become detached, disinterested in the people around them. Cold. Dysfunctional."

"That's... Why doesn't somebody do something about it?"

"We are."

"I mean for real. Police, or scientists, or something?"

"*Excuse me, Constable, but this person has been taken over by a creature from the Beneath, who is making them a nasty person,*"

Evie spoke in a sing song voice, and her eyes were mocking. I leaned away a little. There was so much anger in Evie, and it seemed she didn't always know where to direct it. The waitress chose that moment to come out of the shop, breaking the spell. She carried a tray, and put two tall, thin glasses onto the table, followed by a pitcher of something pink with a foamy top. As though she sensed the tension at the table, she gave each of us a curious glance, but said nothing and departed after offering us another slight bow.

I waited to see if Evie would make the next move, but she was looking down at her hands, gripping the edge of the table so hard that bloodless crescents showed under her fingernails. I grabbed the pitcher and poured a half-glass for each of us. Evie still didn't seem ready to speak, so I lifted my glass and took a suspicious sip of the contents. It was delicious, like a thick strawberry milkshake, but without the threat of brain freeze. I struggled hard with the urge to gulp the rest of the glass down and grab for the pitcher, keeping things down to another controlled sip. I would give Evie one more chance to get it together, then I would ask her to take me home. And I got a surprise by how disappointed that made me feel. "So, can we eat everything here?"

Evie jumped. Her face came up and her expression was one of bewilderment, as though I had kicked her out of a daydream. "What? Oh, yes. Pretty much. Apart from Grenlik food. Think twice before taking *anything* from a Grenlik. Angels, too."

"You have Angels here?"

"Yeah," said Evie, her mischievous grin back. "With Grenlix, you don't know where the food has been, or often what it was. Angel's, you've got to wonder why he's giving you anything."

"So you don't trust Angels?"

"I don't trust anybody. Not even you. I know you're good in a fight, and you don't spook too easily, but apart from that, I don't know who you are."

"So who, what, was the waitress?"

"Hrund. Nice people usually, especially the ladies."

"And I call her Hrund if I don't know her name?"

Evie blanched. "Crap, no. Not unless you want to be thrown out, or over a wall. Everybody else is Sa for females and Ser for males. And don't touch anybody."

"What?"

"Don't touch anybody, even through your clothes, if you can avoid it. Didn't you notice them all getting out of our way?"

"Well, yes, but–"

"It hurts them. All of them. Think of brushing up against a radiator. Just a touch and you pull your hand away and go ouch. Hold your hand against it and you burn, right? I don't know how or why. I do know that not all Underkin are happy when they see one of us walking around, so try to stay out of their way."

The last of the squash went into my glass, and I pointedly ignored Evie's scowl. A low thrumming noise interfered with the conversation, and I looked over my shoulder to see what it was. The street was empty, so I settled for leaning closer across the table.

"So what's this deal you are supposed to be offering me?"

"Exactly what I said. Fast-track Warrior."

"Why?"

"I told you; you're good."

"And the rest of it?"

Evie squirmed in her seat, looking years younger as she realised I had busted her. "How did you know?"

"Styke. She was–" I tried to find a better word but had to settle with my first thought. "Shocked."

Evie nodded. "That's true. It's never been done before."

"Then why?"

"Because there aren't enough of us," Evie said after a pause that made it obvious she didn't want to answer. "Not enough Warriors. More and more Observers bottle out or get locked out before they can graduate. We can't recruit as many kids. People pay more attention, so there's not as much freedom as there used to be. You're a natural. With some training, you'll be near as good as me, and a damn sight better than most."

The thrumming noise was so loud now that I waved my hands next to my ears and shook my head, telling Evie to wait. She pointed upwards, grinning again, and I followed the finger. And gaped like a tourist. An *airship* was coasting majestically overhead. It looked like the Imperial cruiser in the opening of Star Wars, that got bigger, and bigger, and bigger. An engine nacelle went right over us; I couldn't guess how big the propeller was because I couldn't wrap my brain around how big any of it was. The whole nacelle swivelled to point the propeller 45-degrees down, and the thrumming took on a deeper, more purposeful tone as the airship picked up altitude.

"Freighter," Evie yelled. "Probably heading south to Greater Germany."

The rumble faded as the airship turned to port, still rising. I watched it until it left my line of sight, sighed, and turned my attention back to Evie.

"The whole place is like that," said Evie. She couldn't know how big a bribe she had just dropped in front of me. Or maybe, from the way her eyes shone, she did. "Please, just say you'll do the training. Three months. Easter break is around the corner, so it's an easy start and you can pull out whenever you want. Try it."

"How do I find the time? I can't keep disappearing for hours without reason."

"It's not a problem. There are some things I can't tell you. Not until you've joined the program. You'll just have to trust me."

I stood up and pushed my chair back under the table. Evie looked up at me, head tilted sideways, face hopeful. I shrugged as casually as I could.

"Where do I sign?"

Seven

Back at the SFU headquarters, Evie took us in through a different door and up several flights of elegant stairs, until we ended up at the end of an endless corridor, and I ended up out of breath. Like I said, I don't do sports. There was a Hrund on either side of the double doors. I guessed they were male because they both had ridges over their eyebrows and the waitress hadn't. Each wore black knee length smocks with red belts and held a six-foot-long staff. They nodded formally as we passed and, after a perfunctory knock, Evie led us through the doors.

A female Hrund sat behind an oversized desk, on top of which were three neat piles of paper and an oversized manual typewriter. She looked up at Evie, smiled, and gestured towards a row of chairs with an elegant, sweeping hand. "The director will be free in five minutes, Warrior Jones."

"Thank you, Sa," said Evie, nodding her head politely. She pulled me towards the chairs as the secretary's fingers started a staccato tap-dance over the typewriter keys and was whispering in my ear almost before we sat. "We're going in to see the boss. Absolute top dog. Even when he gives you his name, call him Ser. He's Sithaari. They can get pompous. No, they are *always* pompous. Bow when we leave. Piss him off and your life will be miserable forever. And he doesn't like me."

"Why are we going to see him?" I asked.

Whatever Evie had been going to say got lost in the rattle of doors being thrown open and people bustling to leave. There were handshakes all around, mumbled pleasantries, and I tried to remember not to stare. It wasn't easy. There were five in the group, all apparently male. Two looked so ordinary I would have passed them in the street and thought them human. One was taller and more heavily built than the other, and he behaved like he thought himself the senior of the two. They wore old-fashioned clothes, like they were going to a fancy wedding. At least they wore some colour in their bright ties and fancy waistcoats.

The other three looked stretched; tall, thin, and out of proportion. Their faces were long and miserable, and broader at the top than at the chin, so they looked like donkeys. I couldn't figure out if their eyes were too big, or if the nose and mouth were too small. They wore bland frock coats in black with charcoal grey trousers and black boots and looked like undertakers. Evie nudged me. I was staring again. I dropped my eyes, but not quickly enough to miss the calculating look the human-lookalike boss flicked at me, and then the longer stare he directed at Evie.

The group broke up. The secretary, who had emerged from behind her desk as soon as the doors had opened, escorted four of the group out of the office whilst the one who was left disappeared back into the private sanctum. Evie had a calculating look on her face. I nudged her arm and, once she turned to look at me, I raised my eyebrows.

"That was Natrak Sum," she said. "Wonder what he was doing here. He'd have no business—" Evie broke off as the secretary walked back to her desk, then nodded towards the door.

The room was dark and stuffy. Even though there were two tall windows at the far end, the décor seemed to suck up any natural light and only allowed the dim glow of the wall sconces and table lamps to have any effect. Dark, polished wood panelled the walls, which made everything draw in still more.

Furniture crowded the room. The centrepiece was a large desk, easily six feet across, which looked to be made of the same wood as the walls. To one side of the desk were two comfortable chairs, and a couch clustered around a coffee table. On the other was a larger table and six chairs. Evie steered us to two plain chairs in front of the desk, and we came to a halt between them.

The person behind the desk shuffled things around and peered at papers. I wondered that anybody would still try to use such an old trick. It was supposed to make you think you were unimportant, or at least less important than other things the person on the other side of the desk could be doing. I thought it made him look stupid.

"So, Jones. This is the exceptional candidate you have been trying to bully us all about?" The papers stopped shuffling, and he peered at me over a pair of half-moon spectacles.

"Yes, Ser," Evie answered. There was tension in her voice, but I hadn't heard a reason for her to get mad yet. The person behind the desk turned his attention to me.

"My name is Aslnaff. I am the superintendent of the Special Facilities Unit. Jones has persuaded—," he paused, and his mouth puckered into a little moue of disagreement, "—us all that you are sufficiently gifted to be granted an expedited path to the position of Warrior." He paused, sniffed, and used the middle finger of his left hand to push his glasses back up the bridge of his nose. "I remain to be convinced." He enunciated each word extravagantly, biting each off as they left his mouth. "However, the rest of the council seem to find merit in this endeavour, so I am compelled to trial it. You are therefore granted a status of Provisional Warrior, for a period of three months, after which you will be assessed and the continuation of said position and status re-evaluated. You are entitled to the protection due any human member of the SFU, and access to such reasonable equipment as your instructor deems appropriate for your training. Do you agree?"

I nodded before he had finished asking the question, and then was not sure why I'd been so hasty. Surely there were things I should have been asking this man? Person? He slipped a sheet of paper and a pen across the desk towards her. "Sign."

I leaned forward and picked up the pen. Aslnaff's hand was already extended, waiting to take back the signed sheet, but I put the pen to one side and lifted the paper closer so I could read it in the dreadful light. Aslnaff sat back in his chair and I heard him mutter "well, really".

Whoever wrote the form used some high legalese, and I couldn't make sense of ninety per cent of it. The gist seemed to be that they would help me out where and when they could, but that I was in this by my own choice, so if I got hurt, it wasn't their fault. It didn't surprise me. I had to get my parents to sign similar cop-outs when I did just about anything with the school.

I looked at Evie, eyebrows raised, to make sure that this was what she was expecting. She sent back a non-committal shrug. It was sign or walk away, so I reached out for the pen and tried to sign. I got dry scratching and nothing else. Evie coughed and looked pointedly at something on the desk, and I refused to let myself blush as I dipped the pen into an inkwell before trying the signature again. I put the pen down next to the inkwell and handed the paper back to Aslnaff. He tossed it onto a pile without looking at it and turned to Evie.

"Very well, Jones. She's your problem now."

I felt the heat rising in my cheeks again, but Evie grabbed me by the arm and twisted it forward before making a small bow herself. I somehow did the same, then Evie was dragging me towards the door. As soon as we were outside and the doors were closed, Evie gently pushed me against the wall. She seemed to use walls a lot.

"Calm down. He was trying to wind us both up. Take a breath."

"But why?"

"Because he's Sithaari. They're all stuck up and rude, and he's worse than any of them. Maybe just because he can. I warned you he didn't like me. That's why he just called me *Jones*." She was shaking her head now and let go of me. "I can keep myself from blowing up at him, but it's hard. He was really, I mean really, against the whole idea of training you up. It was so cool pushing this past him."

I heard a muffled noise and looked up to see the secretary doing a bad job of trying to control a smile. Were we funny to watch? Silly little humans running around like what they were doing was important? Or was it funny we were showing no respect to the boss? And was I just some kind of trophy Evie was using to annoy Aslnaff? I tugged at my coat. A couple of deep breaths helped, and now all I wanted to do was get out of there. "So what's next?" I asked, speaking to nobody in particular.

"Next," said the secretary, "we add you to the security system. If you would place your hand here?" She gestured to a copper plate mounted on top of an ornate box right at the corner of her desk. I did as she asked. There was a gentle warmth, and the plate glowed with soft yellow light. A moment later, the glow had expanded so that it covered my hand. I was about to jerk it away when the secretary said, "That's fine."

I lifted my hand. The glow seemed to linger around it for seconds, and it wasn't really clear if it faded away or soaked in. I remembered my manners and looked over at the Hrund. "Thank you, Sa."

The secretary smiled. "My pleasure, Warrior Stone."

It had a hell of a ring to it. I kept my face straight until I had my back to the secretary, but then I broke out in a wide smile. I saw Evie wearing the same smile and, for a second, I thought she was mocking me. But I saw there was no malice and figured she must be genuinely pleased. She jerked her chin towards the door and we set off into the bowels of the building again.

"So the tall, thin guys are Sithaari. Who were the others? I mean, they looked so like us."

Evie's face darkened. "They're Angels."

"I thought Angels were good guys."

"Try Angels as in 'of death'. Wherever there is a crooked deal, there's an Angel behind it or at the bottom of it. They're plain nasty. I mean, nobody would trust a Grenlik very far, but Angels are nasty."

"So, there are no people here except us?"

"A few. Very, very few. There are more in the United Americas, I've heard, but not here."

They were back in the locker room, and I asked, "What's next?"

"Getting you home."

"What? But I only just got here. I don't want to go home yet."

"You've been here almost three hours, and I have no idea what your snapback tolerance is yet."

"There you go again with the 'snapback'."

Evie sighed. "It's complicated. There are two ways to get out; jump or snapback. A snapback takes you back to the same time in the Over as when you jumped in, but you can't come back until you've caught up."

That made my brain hurt. My mouth made word shapes, but nothing came out for a moment. "That doesn't make any sense."

"It does if you don't want to meet yourself here. Anyhow, it's time to go home. You'll crash as soon as you get there, I promise."

I opened my locker and put my coat and goggles inside. I was lifting the amulet over my head when I felt Evie's hand on my arm. "Not that. I mean, you're supposed to leave it, but we don't. The rules say no Underworld tech in the Over, and some say it makes jumping more difficult. I don't agree."

"So why do I leave it on?"

"Because sometimes you have to jump in a hurry. You may not have the time to come here, and the Kevlar is your most basic protection. Your *only* protection. Nobody takes them off."

I let the amulet fall from my fingers, then tucked it back inside my top. Questions crowded to be asked and there was so much that still made no sense, but Evie said it was important, so I left the Kevlar on and closed the locker door. Before I could turn away, Evie took hold of my arm. "Stand still, facing your locker. Look at it. Hard. Fix it in your memory. When you come and go, you need to have the picture strong in your mind. If you can fix this in your head, you can save yourself a lot of time walking here from that stupid room with the patterns."

I did as she asked and tried to fix the image of the door in my mind, looking for any catchy little details that might help it stick. It felt like I'd been there five minutes, and I was about to ask Evie how long she had taken to get the hang of jumping, when she pulled me backwards. I fell over her strategically placed leg, pulling me around and twisting me...

...right back to where we had been standing behind Mum's barn. I staggered and took a step sideways before I caught my balance, then glared at Evie. "I wish you'd stop doing that."

"Easier to move you when you aren't expecting it."

A wave of fatigue washed over me and robbed me of any snappy comeback. Evie looked sympathetic. "I tried to warn you."

I opened my mouth to argue, but Evie raised her hand. "No, no more rules or questions tonight. We can start again tomorrow." Tomorrow was Saturday and Claire saw her habitual weekend lie-in fade to a wish.

"When? And where? Here is no good. Mum works in the barn all day and I'm not supposed to hang around unless I'm helping."

Evie thought for a moment. "We need to be somewhere you know really well, but where there won't be too many people."

I grinned. "Do you have a library card?"

Eight

I was sipping an apple juice through a straw when Evie stomped into the café in the corner of the library.

"This is 'not too many people'?" she growled in greeting.

I glanced up from my iPad. Evie towered over me and looked grumpy. She was wearing her usual warrior outfit but without the gadgets. I had dressed more appropriately this time, in a pair of second-best black jeans, a green tee, and my walking boots. "Good morning." I made my voice pointedly bright. "Do you want anything?"

Evie shook her head. "Can we just get on?"

I shrugged, put my iPad away, and finished my juice with a nice loud gurgle. By the time I stood up, Evie had her arms tightly folded and was drumming the fingers of her right hand on her left arm.

"Come with me," I said. I didn't bother keeping that she was annoying me out of my voice.

I led her to the back of the library and down a flight of stairs. They had a seldom-used mustiness about them, which I loved. At the bottom was a very plain door with a panel of frosted glass in the top. The scent of age and infrequent interest got stronger as I pushed the door open. Just inside was a battered desk, equipped with the usual office clutter and a delicate brass bell. I picked it up and gave it a gentle ring.

A distant voice muttered, "Coming, coming," and shuffling footsteps scuffed closer to the desk. A fusty librarian appeared from between two stacks, wild hair and wire-rim glasses pushed up over his forehead.

"Morning, Mr Lee," I said, raising my voice. Mr Lee had hearing issues and never brought spare batteries. His face crinkled into an uncle's smile.

"Good morning, Miss Stone."

"School project. We need to dig around the archive." I mangled the grammar on purpose.

"Dig around *in* the archive," he corrected absently, then nodded. "Of course. Remember to sign yourselves out when you go."

I leaned over the desk. "Will do, Mr Lee." But I only put my name into the register, and I signed myself out an hour in the future. "This way," I muttered to Evie, pointing off into the darkness in the general direction of the newspaper archive.

Automatic strip lights flickered on over our heads as we walked to the back of the room. I saw nobody else and, other than our own footsteps, I heard nothing other than the faint shuffling and muttering of Mr Lee, far in the distance.

"This quiet enough for you?" I asked.

"I guess. Can I get down here on my own?"

"Don't see why not. Just tell Mr. Lee you are working on a project with me."

"Suits me. Ready?"

The sudden switch caught me off guard. "For what?"

"First lesson. I'm guessing you're going to have a problem getting in and out, so you have to practise. It's going to be a pain if I have to fetch you all the time."

I bit back a sarcastic apology for being such a burden. Evie wanted a fight with someone and wasn't too picky about who. I didn't fancy being the target.

"Jumping works differently for everybody. You just have to pay attention when you get taken through, then find a way to make the same thing happen for you. It's kind of like making your mind turn a key in a lock. Or throwing yourself at the ground and missing."

I recognised the quote in an instant, but I'd bet Evie didn't know it came from a book. And I was very sure it wouldn't improve her mood to point out she hadn't invented it. I stood still while Evie came close to me and grabbed my arm, and I tried to concentrate as Evie made the odd little twist in a direction that wasn't there. An instant later, we were in front of my locker. Evie let go and hastily stepped to the end of the row.

"You didn't focus on where you were going," Evie snapped.

"I was trying to see what you did."

"You have to do both."

I sighed and opened my locker. There was more within than when I had last looked. "Santa's been," I said, trying to decide if I liked the delivery service or resented that someone else could get into my locker so easily.

"Krosset must have heard you signed up and shipped in the rest of your kit. You don't need all of it today."

I put on the coat, then rummaged through the new box someone left on my locker's shelf. The utility belt looked fun, but when I lifted it and looked at Evie, she shook her head. Disappointed, I let it fall back in the box. The goggles I put in a pocket, then I found what looked like a torch. The switch was easy enough to find, but I turned it over in my hands, digging at the seams with my thumb nails.

"What are you doing?" Evie asked.

"Trying to figure out where the batteries go."

Evie laughed, but there was a sharp edge to the sound and I felt she was poking fun at me. Still, it was better than snappy and surly.

"It doesn't have batteries," said Evie. "It runs on magic. Like everything else."

I froze, glaring at her. "That's not funny."

Evie raised her hands; defensive and surprised. She didn't expect how angry that made me. It surprised me, too.

"I swear," she said. "Everything here, one way or another, works on magic. Or what they call magic. We'd call it something all scientific, but they call it magic."

"So we have to do spells and stuff to make anything work?"

"We can't do magic—unless you count jumping. Nor can Hrund. Nobody is quite sure about Angels. We just get to use magical stuff."

I was on the edge of telling her to take me home. If she was going to be this much of a cow for the next three months, then it didn't matter how cool it sounded to be a Warrior. It wasn't worth it. But when I looked up, I saw Evie was looking open and honest, and wasn't trying to hide a smirk or a lie.

"But there's no such thing," I said, and it sounded lame as soon as I said it.

Evie shrugged. "It's how things work down here, and it seems to do what they say it does. I'm not going to argue. What I understand is it's like a magnetic field, but magic. Things can store magic like batteries and recharge themselves from the field. They collect heavy duty magic from Outside and tank it into the city for factories and cars and stuff that uses too much to take it from the general field."

"Magic tankers?"

"I'll show you one, someday."

Evie walked down the room to her own locker. I followed and stood next to her as she put on her equipment belt and stashed several small items in various pockets.

"I wouldn't stand there if I were you," Evie commented, casually.

"Why not?" I asked, but Evie had already flattened herself against her locker. My skin tingled all over, then something shoved me sideways. I landed on my backside and slid a couple of yards along the floor. When I looked up to protest, a boy flickered into existence, standing in front of the locker next to Evie's. Evie had her hand covering her mouth, but I knew she was laughing. At me. Again. Although this time maybe she had a reason. The boy looked at Evie, confused, then turned to see me on the floor. He flushed bright red and held out his hand.

"Sorry. Guess you must be new."

I took his hand and let him pull me to up, then we all backed out to the edge of the room.

"My name's Jack. Jack Cooper, Senior Observer." He had his hand out again, this time to shake. I took it briefly. It was warm and dry and he didn't try to crush my hand in his grip, which was nice. I guessed he was about the same age as Evie, just short of six feet tall, and quite slim. He wasn't particularly good looking, and his darkish hair was a disaster, but he had nice, brown eyes and a friendly smile.

"Claire Stone, trainee Warrior," I replied. It still felt weird in my mouth when I said it and from the way his eyebrows shot up, either Jack was surprised or he had already heard of me—which sounds like two sides of the same coin, but you know what I mean.

"Pleasure," he said. "You should watch out for that. Someone jumps into the same space as you, it'll shove you out the way—"

"I was just going through that," Evie interrupted, her tone frosty again.

Jack gave a rueful half smile. "Of course. I'll let you get on with... whatever..." He turned away and walked off.

"That was rude. Is he someone I should be careful around, or something?" I asked.

Evie shrugged. "He's an Observer. Could have been a Warrior but turned it down."

I didn't know what to say. Did that make him a bad person down here, or was it just Evie he had pissed off? I took a safer path and went back to my earlier question. "What are we doing for the rest of the day?"

Evie scratched somewhere under her coat. "Not sure. We should keep it to six hours or so this time. We need to find out where your snapback limit is."

"So we're not going to practise jumping in and out?"

"Not this trip." Evie rubbed her chin and looked thoughtful. It looked contrived, like Evie had known all along there was going to be a 'sudden change of plan". I tried to keep any expression off my face.

Like I read her mind, Evie's face cleared as though she had just had an idea. "I think we should go out for a wander."

NINE

"Anywhere in particular?" I asked.

Evie shrugged. "I dunno. Maybe introduce you to a few people you should know."

We walked a long way down into the building and through another door with a brass security plate. More stairs, and then we stepped out onto a short, narrow, and dimly lit platform. Evie went up to an ornate brass button and pushed it.

"Private station," she explained, yelling into my ear as a train roared through at full speed. "Don't worry, the next one will stop for us."

As promised, the next train squealed to a halt. The cab at the front of the train was empty. The platform was only long enough to take the first car, and only the first pair of doors opened. We got on and Evie took a seat while I stood and studied the map over the doors. I tried to speak over the noise of the train as it picked up speed. "What—?" was all I got out before Evie gave a pointed cough. I looked around and saw we weren't alone. Sharing the carriage with us were a family of Hrund and two Grenlix. The Hrund smiled politely and nodded, whilst the Grenlix made a point of looking anywhere other than at us. I sat next to Evie.

"What line is this?" I asked. "I don't recognise half the station names, and the ones I do know are all in the wrong place."

"Like I said, this place is close enough to the Over to get you confident enough to make a stupid mistake. Just because something seems familiar doesn't mean it is."

We went four stops before Evie stood. I recognised Aldgate and Whitechapel, but "Commercial Road" rang no bells, and neither did "Turner's Road", which was where we got off. The station wasn't deep, and we were on the pavement after a single flight of stairs.

As soon as we came out onto the street, I felt a difference. The area around Tower Hill had been busy, but a mixture of different people. Here, just about everybody I could see was a Grenlik. Carts chugged by pulled along with steam tractors, or hauled by "Grenlik-power", and everything looked worn and suffering from extensive use; paint peeled and repairs were frequent and obvious. An omnibus clattered up the road and made hissing toots at children playing a game of chicken in front of it.

"Nice place," I said, feeling nervous and doing my best not to show it. "Where are we?"

"Doesn't have an official name," Evie replied. "It's sort of halfway between Poplar and Stepney, or would be in the Over. If the Grenlix have a name for it, nobody ever told me. Everybody calls it Turner's Road."

We crossed the road and walked down Cotton Street. It was quieter here, but there was still a hustle of commerce back and forth. It was the buildings that unsettled me the most. I was expecting rows of terraced houses, but there were no houses at all. Only vast structures that looked like warehouses or factories. They were all three floors tall with small, dark windows, and along the street level were alcoves like railway arches. Some were bricked or boarded up, others had small, unwelcoming doors. More than half were open-fronted shops with shutters folded out of the way on either side.

"Are these factories?" I asked.

Evie chuckled, the most relaxed sound she had made all day. "No, that's a Hive. It's what Grenlix call the places they live. I suppose you could say it was like a block of flats, only they go down even farther than they go up."

"Basements?"

Evie shrugged. "Grenlix don't give out info unless they have to, especially not about themselves, and they don't deal with people who betray their secrets. It's something to do with status, but whether up or down is good I wouldn't know. We need to go in here."

We had stopped outside an alcove. It had a more conventional shop front with a door and a display window, but the door was closed and the window was so coated with grime it was impossible to see inside. Everything was slightly scaled down, and the door was only just big enough for me to walk through without stooping. Evie tried the handle, but the door wouldn't budge. She raised a fist and hammered on it.

"Closed!" snarled a voice. "Can't you read?"

I looked around the shop front but couldn't see any sign. Evie hammered on the door again.

"I said closed," the voice said again.

Evie put her lips close to the edge of the door and spoke, her voice not loud but intense. "Get over here and open this door or I'll start—"

I never found out what Evie was threatening to do because there was already a sound of bolts being drawn back and a key turning in a lock. The door swung open into a gloomy interior, and I caught the outline of a diminutive, hunched body moving farther into the unlit depths of the shop. Evie gestured I should step through, and when I hesitated, she gave me a shove. As soon as I moved inside, Evie shut the door behind us and drew one of the bolts.

The ceiling was only a couple of inches above my head, and my shoulders hunched no matter how much I told them the ceiling wasn't going to press down on them. The floor was littered with amorphous shapes concealed by dust sheets. They reminded me of Morphs and I shivered.

There was a strange smell in the air, spicy yet musty, and not pleasant. But it had an edge of mouldiness that caught at the back of my mouth and made me want to cough. I was turning to ask Evie what we were doing here and could I wait outside, when a door at the far end of the room swung open and yellow light lifted the gloom slightly. Evie nudged my arm, and we walked towards the door.

The back room was all workbenches. Assorted unrecognisable devices littered the workbenches in various states of dismemberment and the place was instantly identifiable as somewhere things were mended. Two Grenlix sat on stools at the longest bench, studiously ignoring the humans. I guessed they were young, perhaps apprentices. An older Grenlik stood in the middle of the room, obviously in charge and glaring at me.

Which annoyed me. I'd never done anything to this person, and he was judging me. I pulled myself up and set my shoulders back, pushing away the imaginary weight of the ceiling, and looked coolly back at the proprietor as I bent my head. "Greetings, Grenlik."

To my surprise, some of the hardness went out of the Grenlik's expression, and I got a polite bow in return. "Greetings, Warrior." The Grenlik turned its attention to Evie. "What do you want, Jones?"

"You know what I want, to—," she broke off and flicked a guilty look at me. "You know what I want, Grenlik. Is it ready yet?"

Evie didn't get a straight answer. "Who is she?" asked the Grenlik, jerking its head towards me.

"A new recruit. I'm training her."

The Grenlik looked even more suspicious—or that's how it looked to me—but Evie didn't offer anything else. Eventually it turned back to me and gave another little bow. "Grenlik Krennet Tolks."

"Warrior Claire Stone," I replied, and everybody in the room seemed to breathe out.

"So?" said Evie, and I thought she sounded like a ten-year-old at Christmas, hoping she got the bike she wanted.

"It's ready," Tolks admitted with an air of reluctance. "But it is not good, it is not proper."

"But it does work?"

"In a manner. The accuracy is... disappointing."

"It will have to do. I've been waiting for months for one to turn up."

I flicked my attention from one to the other like I was watching tennis and didn't understand a word. There was a pause as Tolks tried to find another argument, but his shoulders sagged in defeat.

"Very well, Jones. But I take no blame for this, and I did not provide the device."

My eyebrows shot up, and I tried to catch Evie's eye. It wasn't until Tolks turned and walked away through another door that Evie looked back.

"He's the best," she said. "Anything you need found, or anything you need fixing, Tolks can find it or mend it."

"What's he doing for you?"

Evie's eyes slid away. "Oh, just a gadget I've been trying to find."

"And this is honest? On the level? Nobody says, 'you didn't get it from me' unless there's something hooky about it."

Evie laughed, but it sounded fake. "That's because he's not happy with the accuracy, not because it's bent."

I let the lie lie, but I didn't believe Evie, and I'd made my point. Tolks reappeared, carrying something wrapped in a cloth, which he handed to Evie. Without unwrapping it, she tucked it away in a pocket before shaking hands with the Grenlik.

And that was it. No small talk, no leave-taking. The Grenlik simply turned his back on us and walked away, while Evie gave me a gentle push back towards the door.

Ten

The next time I opened my locker I found someone had left me even more new toys while I'd had been away, not the least of which was a weapon identical to the one she had used to rescue Evie, complete with a holster. It sat in a series of clips on the back wall of the locker, and all I had to do was grab hold of it and pull.

"Do they always dig around in our lockers like this?" I asked.

Evie shrugged. "Grenlix manage Stores. You couldn't keep them out if you tried."

"But it's not very private."

"Would you leave anything valuable or secret in your school locker?"

"No. Well, not for long."

"Exactly. Besides, Grenlix have this weird honour thing. They'd never steal from us because they work for us, and they'd never open your locker without the right paperwork." She paused and looked thoughtful. "Of course, if they *didn't* work for us... Anyway, want to try it out?"

I nodded, making a mental note never to leave anything personal or embarrassing in the locker.

Evie took me down into the basement again, into a space big enough for three or four tennis courts. Rails crisscrossed all over the ceiling, and in the corner sat a little engine, hissing to itself and venting little puffs of steam. The area around the entrance was well lit, but the rest of the space was divided into pools of light. Evie stood in front of me and held her own weapon up in her hand.

"This is your basic Mk 22 Anti Incursion Weapon. It has an up-rated absorption chamber for faster recharging in weak magical fields, and projects a cloud of flechettes with an imbued property of being able to disrupt the surface tension of Morphs. We call it a PPG." She spoke in a fast singsong, like she was reciting something.

"A what?" I got about half of it and understood nothing.

Evie grinned. "We call them Purple Puff Guns."

She turned a valve on the engine in the corner and it chugged with greater enthusiasm, its little piston spinning a flywheel on a shaft that disappeared into the wall. Targets hanging on metal rods scooted around the tracks on the ceiling. Thin sheets, like cardboard, painted as figures or targets. And there were things that looked like punching bags.

Evie started me off aiming at the small targets. A hit glowed for a few seconds then faded away, and on the far wall two counters kept score. Evie went into the lead straight away and scored twenty first. A harsh buzzer sounded, and everything stopped moving. I only scored twelve and was not pleased.

"Level 2?" Evie asked. I had no idea what 'level 2' entailed, but I shrugged agreement anyway. Evie fiddled with something by the engine and the targets all scurried back to where they started from. Two Morph-shapes, one coloured red, the other blue, slid into place in front of us, and the score counters both clicked down from five. At the last instant, Evie shouted, "Catch it if you can". She ran off after her target, which had slid off down the hall.

The target in front of me also shifted. I ran after it, bringing the PPG up for a running shot. Just as I got an aim, one of the punch bags knocked me from my feet and sent me rolling across the floor. I sat up, furious at Evie for not warning me, but then I saw how intricate the game was, and it caught my curiosity. Padded bags tried to knock me over, other targets kept blocking my line of sight, and if I stayed still too long, something would come after me.

I looked up at my scoreboard. Minus 10! Already! A cardboard Grenlik zoomed towards me and I rolled out of its way, coming to my feet as part of the same motion. Another quick look around and I spotted my target near the far end of the room. I as I ran towards it, I zapped a Morph coming in from my left, and dodged a smiling Hrund lady with a child.

Two more passing Morphs got zapped, then I managed a hit on my personal nemesis. I flicked a look up to the scoreboard. I was almost level with Evie. My grin got wider and my eyes narrowed. This was fun, even if I was gasping for breath and glowing in a very unladylike way.

The buzzer sounded to mark the end of the level. I had no idea how much time had passed and had even less sense of what my score might be. I hoped I kept up at least halfway with Evie, and that she didn't brag too much about beating me. A bag knocked over again, but I saw Evie rolling across the floor at least twice, so I didn't feel so bad. I stood up, found Evie, and walked over to her. She was breathing hard and didn't look happy. What had to happen to keep this girl smiling?

"How did we do?" I asked, trying to keep my voice light and neutral. Evie said nothing, but jabbed her chin in the general direction of the score board. I turned, and my jaw dropped. It had to be a mistake. There was more information than before, but it looked like I beat Evie. Only by two points, but that would be enough to explain the foul expression on Evie's face.

There was one pair of numbers, coloured red, where Evie had scored more than me, so I figured I had to be safe talking about those. "What are the red ones? You got a fair few more of them than me."

Evie turned to face me and glared. "Shooting the wrong target," she said in an icy voice, and walked over to fiddle with the engine. When I wandered over, Evie turned on me. "What's the time?"

"I... uh..." I didn't have a clue. Not even close. I raised my arm to look at my watch, but it wasn't there, and that was the moment I remembered I decided not to wear it in case it got scratched. My parents got it for me last Christmas.

"What time was it when you jumped in?"

"I don't know that either," I replied, keeping my voice calm. Evie was brewing for a fight again.

"You have to," she snapped. "You always need to be aware how long you have been down here. What if you had stayed over your snapback time? It could be midnight in the real and the only place you can jump out to is the library, and that's closed."

"What?" I said, panicking. My parents would be worrying, and after the disaster with the movie episode, I really didn't...

"Relax. I said, "what if". You still have time to snap back."

"Then why did you say it?" I said, struggling not to get mad. "That scared me."

"It was meant to. I wanted you to think about what might have happened."

I stared at my PPG for a moment, trying to push aside the image of shooting it at Evie, then very carefully made sure the safety was on before I slipped it back into its holster. "Why not show me a snapback and we can call it a day?" I knew I sounded frosty, but I meant to.

Evie, unapologetic, looked me in the eye for a moment before turning away. She said nothing on the walk back to the locker room, or while we stored our gear away. When she came to stand next to me, I stiffened.

"It's not much of a difference," she explained. "But you have to think of *when* you are going as much as *where*. You didn't check the time, so you can't practise, but you can watch me."

Evie took my arms, and I felt the peculiar turn in and direction that wasn't really there, but this time there was an extra pull I hadn't felt before. Then we were back in the archives of the library. Evie let go and stepped away as soon as I had my balance, then seemed to wait for something.

"Aren't you going back?" I asked.

"Can't. We snapped back two hours and five minutes. I can't jump back in for that long."

I was about to ask why when I figured it out myself. "Or you would be there twice?"

Evie nodded.

"Suppose we better leave the hard way, then."

I led her out into the mid-afternoon sunshine. Around us, the mall was busy but not manic and my throat felt dry. "Want a smoothie or something," I suggested, wondering if Evie would accept and not sure if I wanted her to or not.

She shrugged. "Why not?"

I knew a smoothie bar where you could get the most astonishing range of bizarre things turned into milkshakes. A fairly mundane double-banana was all I wanted, but after several minutes of agonising over three different types of candy, Evie plumped for something involving a chocolate crème egg and a honeycomb bar. Even the machine operator looked impressed by the combination, although it left me wondering about the rest of her diet. We took seats at small metal tables outside the shop and watched the world go by.

The silence felt awkward and Evie didn't seem about to chat, so I tried to kick-start something. "I just realised you could be from anywhere."

Evie finished a long, and by the way the straw caved in quite difficult, pull from her drink and savoured it for a moment before answering.

"Yup."

I tried again. "But you must live pretty close. I mean, your accent is London-ish. Not that I'm any good at that sort of thing."

"No, close enough. Around Cheswick."

That was about ten miles south; a medium-sized 'new town' with an undistinguished reputation. Not rough, or nasty, but not nice either. I gritted my teeth, thought about blood and stones, and tried one more time.

"What does your dad do?"

Evie stopped in mid suck and her lips unglued from around the straw with a soft "pop". She lifted her head and stared straight into my eyes. I dropped my head. The contact was too intense.

"What's with the twenty questions routine?"

"Sorry. I was just chatting."

"You were poking."

"All right, maybe I was," I admitted, feeling my face flush. "I don't know anything about you. You know where I live, what my mum does. Loads."

Evie stared at me a little longer. Her eyes were still piercing, but some of the hostility had faded. Abruptly, she looked down at the table and took another drag on her viscous milkshake.

"My dad left us when I was three, or so my mum said. She didn't take it too well, and by the time I was eight, I was in care. Still can't get a straight answer if they took me or she gave me up. Been there ever since. Still there. Expect they'll kick me out in a year or so. As soon as I finish sixth form at college, anyway. That enough?"

I mumbled something that sounded something like 'sorry" and wondered if I could make an excuse, dump the remaining half of my milkshake and leave. This was too much information, too deep and too raw. But, if I tried to drink the milkshake any faster, I would get a biblical brain freeze. I was rummaging around in my pockets, checking for my mobile and return ticket, or pretty much anything other than trying more conversation, when Evie let out a deep sigh.

"I'm sorry. I'm not good with people, so I always think that someone asking questions is after something. My mum left me long before I went into care. Years before. I thought it was because of my dad. She seemed to turn in on herself and away from me, and I thought she couldn't handle being on her own, or that it was my fault, or all the usual bullshit the psychiatrists try to make you think of when they 'analyse' you. So they took me into care, and only a couple of weeks later someone recruited me, and it was then I realised that my mum had been infected by a Morph."

My eyebrows shot up even though I tried to stop them, and I bit down on my tongue to stop myself from blurting out anything unhelpful. My first instinct was to argue, or to at least suggest there were an awful lot of other answers before we got to Morphs, but there was a look on Evie's face that told me that would be a waste of time. It was the look I'd seen on the faces of televangelists when I'd been studying 'World Religions'.

"I knew I had to do everything I could to help in Underland; to be the best Warrior they had ever had. Maybe one day even find a way to get the Morphs out of people in the Over."

"Do you still see your mum?"

Evie shook her head. "She's not interested, but Smeggie Nicks says they have an address for her when I'm ready for it."

"Who?"

Evie giggled, the first cheerful sound I heard from her since PPG practise. "Meg Nixon, our shelter supervisor. We all call her 'Smeggie Nicks'. She's all right, though." She drew on the straw again, but her only reward was an intestinal gurgle. "Finished. As am I. See you later."

"Where? When? Tomorrow?"

Evie thought for a moment. "No. You'll be tired later today. Try to stay up until your normal bedtime, though. You'll be tired tomorrow too. Monday. Same place. Ten o'clock."

I nodded and, with a nonchalant wave, Evie strode off.

Eleven

"How much trouble am I in?" I asked as we walked along Lower Thames Street. It was early evening, and the neutral yellow sky was fading towards ochre. For the last two weeks, I met Evie every other day. Tracking, target practice, and traipsing around the broken copy of central London had taken most of the training time. That, and practising jumps. Even though Evie swore she could feel me pulling away from her, I still couldn't make my own way in or out.

"None," Evie said, turning her head to smile. "Some take to it easier than others. I told you."

"But the ones that can't do it. How are they weeded out?"

"Used to be if they couldn't jump in on their own that was as far as they got, then they relaxed it so that you could get help jumping in, but you had to jump out on your own. Eventually."

"How long is "eventually"?"

She stopped and turned to face me. "Look, stop obsessing about it. It's like most things; the more you stress yourself out, the more difficult it gets. They gave us three months to train you. You've only used two weeks."

"But it's not usual. To take this long, I mean."

Evie growled, threw up her arms and walked off. I had to jog for a few steps to catch up. I wasn't surprised. Evie had been getting easier to upset for the past week. Half the time she seemed lost in a world of her own. Maybe the training was more than she bargained for, but I let it drop. Maybe she was right, and the best thing to do was to ignore it. I poked her in the arm as I drew level.

"Where are we going?"

"Observer Station," Evie replied.

"Is it far?"

Evie pointed ahead of us, and up. A slender tower sprouted from the top of a tall building about four hundred yards away. I squashed a groan. Heights were not my thing.

The building was anonymous. There were no signs or names over the letterboxes, and someone left the door unlocked. There was an ancient elevator, and I insisted on pulling the old-style metal grilles across and working the lever to make it go up. It wheezed and rattled so much I decided to take the stairs back down.

The carpet along the top floor corridor had holes worn through and the paint on the woodwork peeled on every surface. Evie led me to the far end and opened a door without knocking. Behind was a very ordinary office, except staffed by teenagers. Everybody in the room looked up in surprise as we entered. Most turned right back to what they were doing, but a few stared; a mixture of expressions ranging from awed to disdainful. In one corner a Warrior sprawled on a couch. He acknowledged us, but also made no attempt to hide his curiosity.

A fussy looking girl, who looked a year or so younger than me and instantly reminded me of Melanie Styke, rose from a desk and walked across the room. "Warriors are not supposed to be at an observation post unless it's their duty position."

I felt Evie bristle like a sudden static field made the hairs on her arm prickle, and I pretty much agreed. "Familiarization visit," said Evie, voice tight and terse.

"We weren't notified, so you'll have to—"

A door to the left opened and a young man walked across the room. "I'll deal with this, Sooz."

"But they're supposed to—"

"I said I'll handle it." It was the boy from the locker room, and I struggled to remember his name. He looked pointedly at 'Sooz' and raised his eyebrows. Sooz held her position for a moment longer then stomped back to the desk she had been sitting behind.

"Sorry about that," said Jack—I remembered right as he spoke. "Can I help you?"

He was looking at me, not at Evie, and my cheeks pinked up. His hair looked different to how I remembered; spikier, as though he had gelled it. It looked better.

"Like I said, I wanted to show her an Observation post." Evie's voice still had an edge, but she sounded less hostile.

"Sure," said Jack. "Want the full tour?" He was still looking at me, not her.

I glanced at Evie to see how I should answer, but had a calculating look on her face, and I think she was considering something else.

"Tell you what, Jones-"

Evie's attention snapped back to the now. "That's *Warrior* Jones."

Jack's eyes started to roll, but he stopped them. "Sorry. *Warrior* Jones. Anyway, what I was going to say was would you like to leave Warrior...?"

"Stone," I supplied.

"With me for a couple of hours? I can give her the tour, explain the procedures, and so on."

"Yeah. OK."

I almost gave myself whiplash turning my head.

"I have something I need to do for a bit, and you'd only be bored," Evie explained, but she didn't look me in the eyes as she spoke. "If Cooper doesn't mind you under his feet for a couple of hours, it might be a good idea."

"Not at all," said Jack, a little too quickly, and I turned back to him with eyes narrowed. As soon as I looked away, Evie turned and walked out of the room, throwing a, "see you" over her shoulder at me as the door closed behind her. I was uncomfortably aware that every eye in the room was on me again.

"So, ah, what goes on at an observation post?" I asked, then winced as I realised how lame I sounded.

"If you did things right, you'd know," muttered a voice behind me, and I jumped as Jack barked "Enough," glaring at someone over my shoulder before inviting me over to the other side of the room with a gesture. Tucked into a corner was a battered desk, with a chair either side and a pile of papers at one end. At the other end were two mugs, one of which looked like it had been there for a while, a bag with half a sandwich in it, and a battered copy of "Friday" by Robert Heinlein lying open and spine up. Behind and to the side of the desk was an enormous map that covered most of the wall. I strolled up to it and peered. It was exquisitely detailed and, so far as she could tell, hand drawn.

"Beautiful, isn't it?" said Jack. I jumped. He was standing right next to me and I forgot he was there. I took the chair on the far side of the desk, and Jack told me about the day-to-day workings of an Observation Post.

It wasn't that he was a boring speaker. His voice didn't have that horrible jobsworth drone like teachers dragging their way one term closer to their retirement, but the subject was about as inspiring as crop rotation or Corn Laws of 1815. Rotas, maximum watch times, certifications, warrior locations, use of runners depending on age and enough detail to make my eyes glaze over after twenty minutes. I tried so hard to look interested, fidgeting from side to side, pushing a fingernail into the cuticle of my thumb. Every trick of the bored student trying hard not to fall asleep, and all of no use when I realised Jack had stopped talking and was looking at me with a crooked smile.

"It is a bit much to take in all at once," he said.

I nodded, afraid my boredom had been too obvious and I'd had offended him, but he looked bright enough and was smiling.

"How about we go up and see where it's all done?"

"On the roof?"

"And up the tower."

"I don't know. I'm not that good with heights."

"Perfectly safe. Trust me?"

"No," I replied, but I smiled to take any nasty out of the words.

Jack led me to another door, on the other side of the room. "Up top if anybody wants me," he said to anybody who was listening, and there was a muted mutter of acknowledgement as he opened the door and invited me to climb the flight of stairs on the other side.

The roof was flat and had a low brick wall around it. I thought we were already quite high enough, and that the wall looked quite inadequate. The view was panoramic. To the east I saw the Tower of London, and to the west Hyde Mountain dominated the skyline. Then I turned around and saw the wooden observation tower. I wasn't sure how tall it was, but it was too tall. With ladders up between the legs, it looked entirely too narrow to support the platform at the top.

"I am not going up that."

"It really is safe," said Jack, putting what he must have thought looked like an encouraging smile.

"I don't think I care."

He chuckled, but instead of trying to persuade me further he turned to the tower and shouted up at it, hands cupped around his mouth. "O'Malley. Drop something. Something big."

There was a brief pause then a silhouette marred the straight lines of the platform's edge. A moment later something the size of a child's head flew outwards from the platform. I shifted my weight ready to step out of harm's way, but whatever it was slowed down, rather than speeding up, and drifted inwards towards the tower. It came to a gentle halt on the roof, right at the foot of the first ladder.

"Safety net," said Jack, grinning. "Every tower has one. Magical, obviously. Now, are you sure you won't come up?" He picked up the bag and hooked an arm through it. "I have to take this back up or O'Malley will moan for days. Honestly, you have to see it to believe it."

I desperately wanted to say *no*, but this was now about saving face. They all thought it was safe. I was supposed to be a Warrior, and I didn't want to be known as the one who wouldn't go up a tower. I clenched my jaw and nodded. Jack beamed a smile and stood back. "You first, then I can help if you need anything."

I reached out with shaking hands and took hold of the rung in front of my eyes. Liquid tingles ran down the back of my legs and my heart hammered uncomfortably in my ears.

I stared at the ladder, refusing to look beyond it or, worse, down from it, and climbed. I counted rungs, but somewhere around twenty the numbers slipped away as I concentrated on the sequence hand-hand-foot, gripping so hard I was afraid I'd leave dents in the wood.

Eventually, I sensed the looming bulk of the platform above me, and then the floor passed in front of my eyes. Helpful hands reached out to haul me the last few feet, and I got an impromptu round of applause. Jack clattered up behind me, and the trap door slammed shut.

"Well done," he said. "Not everybody can make it up here, and few Warriors ever bother. People will talk about you."

"I think they already are," I said, earning a chuckle from all three observers. Apart from Jack, there was a girl of around twelve, and a boy perhaps a year older. Both were wearing goggles, but different to mine. They were bigger, with wider lenses that had thick wires coiled around their edges, like the coils on my Kevlar amulet. They stood at the edge of the platform and scanned their heads from side to side like radar dishes.

"Want to see *our* world?" Jack asked, holding a pair towards me.

Twelve

I'm not sure why I hesitated before I took the goggles from Jack's hand. As I raised them to my face, I caught a hint of citrus and the seaside, and guessed they were Jack's own. I approved of his taste in aftershave, not that he looked like the shaving part was too much of a problem yet.

As the goggles settled over my eyes everything went black, and again there was a ripple of shifting colour before the lenses cleared. The view was very dark, almost black, and I could see enough to move.

"Let me help," Jack said, softly and too close to my ear. A little shiver tickled between my shoulder blades which I was certain was down to being in the dark atop the tower. Almost. But I was sure it wasn't because that was the closest a boy had ever stood to me. If you know what I mean. "They can be scary the first time you put them on."

I felt a gentle hand on my arm lead me forwards, the top of the wall around the platform pressed against me, just below my ribs, and I gasped. "Oh, wow."

UnderLondon spread out beneath me in a mesh of soft, dark blue, sparkling like Tinkerbell's contrail. Lighter local hotspots were scattered here and there, but the structure of London was reduced to silhouettes against an ultramarine background. Tiny streaks of bright scarlet like individual raindrops of fire shot downwards at random intervals. "It's so beautiful. What are you looking for?" I asked.

"Incursions," said Jack. "If you're really good, you can see a change in the background a few seconds before, but most of the time we only see when an incursion is in progress. Then you know it. It's like a pillar of fire, white or yellow, shooting up from the ground. The trick is in figuring out where it's coming from when all you have is shadows of buildings."

"And the little red sparks?"

There was a pause. "Pardon?"

"The little red sparks coming down?"

There was a slightly longer silence than there should have been, and Jack's voice didn't sound quite right as he turned me away from the rail. "Perhaps that's enough for now. These goggles can take some getting used to. The sparks are probably just your eyes adjusting to the magic, or the other way around."

I heard a lie in his voice. Not a huge one, and more about protecting me than hiding something. The door on the roof opened, distracting us both and taking away my opportunity to dig deeper. Voices and the crunch of footsteps on the gravel drifted up from the roof, then feet clattered on the ladder. The two observers already on the platform removed their goggles, waved, and jumped over the edge. I squealed, then remembered the magical safety net and felt stupid.

"It's quicker," Jack explained. "This platform is only rated for four people. And maybe a bit of showing off for the visitor. Officially, I should be grumpy about it, but it doesn't hurt anyone."

The two new observers took up posts with barely a nod to me or Jack, and I realised we were in the way. It was an impressive sight, but one that I'd seen enough of and there was still the problem of getting down again.

It took a while, but I managed to get my feet back down to the roof. Conflicting feelings of being on something much firmer, but still way too high, left me dizzy until we went back down the stairs. Evie hadn't returned, and we were in that awkward place where I should have left but couldn't.

"Has Warrior Jones shown you about much," Jack asked as they sat at his desk.

I nodded, then twisted my lips to one side. "Sort of. We've done a lot of tracking old incursions. That's got us around a bit."

"But all business?"

I nodded.

"That sounds like Jones," said Jack, with a wry smile, then an idea seemed to occur to him. Whatever it was, I saw indecision on his face. "Look, I'm due off shift now anyway. How would you like to see a couple of the real sights, not work stuff?"

"I don't think so," I replied, slowly. Jack's face fell and he looked embarrassed. "Not because it doesn't sound interesting, but–" and it was my turn to hesitate. This was not an admission I wanted to make in public, but Jack had been very kind and I owed him the truth. I leaned forward across the desk. He did the same, and I lowered my voice. "I can't jump in or out on my own yet. Evie, I mean 'Warrior Jones', picks me up and drops me back."

Jack sat back in his chair with an "Ah" of understanding. "Awkward." He mused for a minute, and a smile gradually climbed up his face. "Sod her. She wandered off to do something else and didn't say when she'd be back. Let's bunk off for a couple of hours. She can either wait here or leave a message where to meet her."

I thought about how pissy Evie could get, and how likely it was this would set her off, then thought about how Jack was right and things had been very much work and very little play. I made up my mind, and grinned back. "Why not."

Fifteen minutes later we were on the street and heading for the nearest underground station. "I don't know if this sort of thing will get to you," Jack explained. "It certainly gets to me, and if it doesn't float your boat, it'll give me a better idea of the things you do like." Beyond that, he would offer nothing more in explanation, and exacted a promise that I would do what he said no matter how weird it got. I had to think hard about that one. There were stories about people who asked for commitments like that, but Jack didn't seem the type, and all I was doing was promising. I could still bail if anything got too uncomfortable.

We got off at a station called "Broad Street". Again, not one that I recognised, but there was something she thought she ought to remember about the name. As soon as they got off the train, Jack asked her to keep her eyes on the ground. It was a surface level station, so there weren't many steps, but when they were in the ticket hall, Jack upped the stakes.

"I want you to shut your eyes and let me lead you. One flight of stairs and a dozen paces either end."

In a public place? There would be Grenlix and Sathaari and Hrund all around us, so I would be safe, if perhaps embarrassed. I nodded, closed my eyes and felt his hand take my arm. I didn't count the steps, but it felt about right. At the bottom of the stairs the sound changed from an enclosed space to something cavernous.

"Look straight ahead, and open your eyes," said Jack.

My eyes opened, and kept going, while my chin dropped in a soundless gasp. I didn't know where to look, overwhelmed by the sheer number of things to see. The space we were in was beyond vast, and could have accommodated a couple of cathedrals. As if that wasn't astonishing enough, directly in front of me was an airship. Beside it, another. The gasbags were the size of blue whales, and the gondolas hanging beneath were bigger than a train carriage. Somewhere a whistle sounded; not a little "toot toot" but a resounding blast that said it meant business and that something important was about to happen. Jack tapped me on the shoulder and pointed at a space on the roof, farther back than the two airships and off to the left.

The whistle sounded again, followed by a metallic screech as some enormous gears engaged. Far above there was a loud clunk, followed by much grinding. A crack formed in the roof, and I watched a pair of enormous shutters fold open.

With another thump the doors stopped moving, and the whistle gave two short blasts. From behind the airships blocking my view, I heard huge propellers beat and, with ponderous grace, a behemoth eased itself into the air. At first, I thought two airships were rising at the same time, but then I realised they were bound together. Tail surfaces flapped up and down, back and forth, as though they were undergoing one last check, then the bottom of the gasbags came into view. Beneath each was a gondola that looked as big as an airplane cabin. Three engine pods stuck out from either side, pointing downwards to ease the monster into the air. As it passed through the roof, there was the slightest ripple in the outer skin as the wind stroked against it, showing the outline of the ribs beneath . An even deeper thrum beat down into the cavernous hanger, and as the airship moved off, I saw the three massive propellers at the back of the vessel beating the air to drive the airship forward.

"Daily shuttle to Petit Paris," said Jack, just loud enough to be heard. "I thought we might be in time to see her go."

I nodded, awestruck, still looking up as the roof doors rumbled closed.

"You like?" Jack asked. I nodded again, still speechless. "My kind of geek," he said with a satisfied nod.

The two hours we allotted ourselves passed in minutes, and our excursion went no further than Broad Street Terminus. When I'd had my fill of airships, there were the rail platforms along which smokeless steam trains pulled freight and passenger cars out to who knew where. A brief break for a squash, and it was time to head back to the Observation station at Eastcheap. Outside the front door, I caught Jack's arm and pulled him to one side. "I need a favour."

"If I can."

"If this works, can you tell Evie—I mean Warrior Jones—usual place and time, day after tomorrow." I took my PPG from its holster and handed it to him.

Jack took the weapon like I had handed him a dead rat, but checked the safety with an automatic movement and a casual competence that made me look twice.

"Why, what are you—?"

I had already taken two steps back from Jack. I smiled at him, and was pulling in my will, focusing my thoughts on the stacks of the archives, thinking of myself looking at the wall clock at 10:22. There was no Evie, no pressure. Nothing to stop me except myself. I held everything inside, drew in a breath to go with it, and turned directly into a high table holding back issues of the Hertfordshire Mercury. I put out my hands to steady myself and started to laugh.

Thirteen

Two days later, I tried the same trick to jump in, only this time I focused on the front of my locker. I was already wearing my warrior gear. It had the approval of my parents, impressed with my "new look". Even got me an offer of a mother-daughter shopping trip to buy me some really imposing boots. But nothing happened. When I jumped, I felt a sense of anticipation, but this morning I felt nothing except worry, then failure. I sighed, picked up my student travel pass, and started walking to the bus stop.

Evie was, as usual, late and jumped into the archives so close to me she shoved me sideways. She just glared at me for a moment, her expression indecipherable apart from a slight frown, then she grimaced and shrugged. "Think you can do it again?"

It was a challenge, more than a question.

"I don't know."

"If you can, one rule. Apart from your Kevlar, never, *ever*, take any Underland technology out into the Over."

"OK" I decided it would be best not to mention the phone in my pocket, or the torch or the goggles.

"Come on, then."

"I still can't jump in. I already tried today."

Evie took my arms and jumped us, hard, into the locker room. "Now, can you jump out again?"

I tried, but it was like when I had been at home. I felt nothing except tension, anxiety. My eyes start to fill. "I'm *never* going to get the hang of this."

Evie said nothing, but when I glanced at her, she looked embarrassed. I hoped it wasn't because I'd almost lost it.

"You know, it could be me," said Evie. "I could be putting you off, making you nervous."

I sniffed. The thought had crossed my mind, several times, but I'd never found the nerve to suggest it. Evie was so confident, so imposing, that I felt I could never measure up. So I nodded, like the idea had only just occurred to me. "Might be."

A shadow of disappointment, and perhaps hurt, flickered across Evie's face, and there was an uncharacteristic slump to her shoulders. I felt bad and hadn't meant to hurt her.

"No," Evie pulled herself up. "The more I think of it, the more I think it might be a good idea. Give you a different perspective on things. There must be another Warrior I can ask." The last came out quieter, slower, as if she wasn't sure there was.

"Or an Observer?" I said, then wished I'd kept my mouth shut. Evie gave me a very direct look and my cheeks burned. "I only meant that another Warrior would be just as intimidating." No matter what I said, it would sound lame.

"Let's think about it," said Evie. "For now, target practice, then tracking."

It felt like punishment, and I groaned.

Six hours later we called a halt. Evie allowed me one brief break, but otherwise she kept me busy the whole time and wore me out. We had just walked into the locker room when there was a chirping noise, and something buzzed in my pocket.

"Are you going to answer that?" asked Evie, looking intrigued.

"Answer what?" I said. My phone was in my locker, switched off, but then I remembered I had my Underland phone. So far,

I hadn't used it. Now, it seemed someone was calling me. I took it from my pocket. "Hello?" It tingled in my hand as it made the connection.

"Claire? It's Jack. Jack Cooper? I remembered you said you might be in Underland today. Wondered if you knew what time you were finishing?"

I turned away from Evie's arch look, my face flaming and wishing the call was more private. "Why?"

Jack's voice lost all its confidence. "Well, I thought you might like to spend an hour or two looking around the place some more. Maybe doing some map work and going through some of the major differences between Underland and the Over."

I turned back to Evie and raised my eyebrows. Evie frowned, then snapped "Whatever" before turning and marching out of the locker room. My eyebrows climbed higher. What had I done wrong now? I was torn between chasing after Evie to see what the matter was and letting her stomp off and get whatever it was out of her system. I must have thought about it longer than I realised.

"Claire?" Jack's voice sounded concerned now. "Is everything OK?"

"Sounds good to me. Where are you?"

Stepping alone onto the streets of Underland was a very different feeling. I still wore my uniform, even down to the PPG holstered along my leg, but I felt a fraud. As I walked up to the Lower Thames Street checkpoint, the two guards—both Hrund—watched me. I saw judgement in their eyes and I slowed down, my confidence evaporating with every step. I stopped, ready to turn and run back to the locker room.

One of the Hrund stepped forward, stood to attention in front of me and gave a sharp bow. "Warrior, is there something I can do for you? You seem... distracted."

I nodded politely back, but what should I do? The Hrund was looking at me, expecting an answer. But he had called me Warrior and saluted me. That made me stand up straight.

"Thank you, Ser. I was deep in thought. I'm grateful for your concern."

The Hrund smiled, gave me another bow, and returned to his post. I gave him a couple of steps so it didn't look like I was following him and walked towards the gate. In a moment, I was out on the street.

I knocked on the door to the observation post before I opened it and walked into chaos. Jack, the sour girl Sooz, and a Warrior were clustered around the map while a younger observer, looking very pale and shocked, sat in Jack's chair answering questions. "Is this a bad time?"

"We've got an incursion," Jack threw over his shoulder at the same moment as the sour girl glared at her. "Give me a minute."

There were more hurried questions, a brief argument over a specific point on the map, and the Warrior strode purposefully towards the door. He took out his PPG, checking the safety, the pointy bit, and the charge crystal, then he patted his Kevlar and covered his eyes with his goggles. The door slammed behind him and the room was silent.

People returned to whatever they were doing. Jack sat at his desk, running a hand up through already dishevelled hair. "Sorry about that."

"No problem. Want to leave it for today?"

Jack pursed his lips and puffed air. "No, don't think so. In fact, want to go through the process?"

"Sure." I wasn't sure why I was so pleased Jack hadn't taken up my offer to bail. He went through how the observer who made the visual would hammer down the stairs to the office, then they would discuss where on the map the incursion flare seemed to come from, then the duty warrior would head out to find the trail and follow it.

"So your Warrior is already out, what happens then?"

"Runners. One to the nearest observation post, one to the office. And we put our flag up to say we are dealing with an incident."

It was my turn to frown. "That's got so many holes in it," I complained. "How often does it go wrong?"

Jack pulled a face. "More often than I like, and way more than we admit. Are you OK?"

I felt something in my head, like something made my mind stretch out like a sigh, and I was dizzy for a moment. It passed in seconds and I put up a hand to stop Jack, who was already halfway around the desk with his hands out to catch me. He still took my arm, and it felt nice. For the first time, I understood what my mum meant when she talked about 'feeling grounded'.

"I'm fine—" was as far as I got before the sound of running feet echoed down from the roof. Somebody was shouting, and Jack's face went pale. "Another one?" I asked, and all Jack could do was shrug.

They pushed aside me as another observer joined Jack and a new huddle formed around the map. Amid all the fuss, a quiet-looking girl of about twelve picked up her coat and headed out the roof door, presumably to make sure there was enough coverage on the platform.

"It was right on top of us,"

"Be specific."

"I mean it. I saw it on the ground. Right at the end of Eastcheap. It headed south."

"Shit. It could head for the river, or for one of the docks. Send runners to the Tower. Who else is available?" asked Jack.

"St. Swithins, Leadenhall and the Tower are all running flags. They may have sent out warriors against the last one."

"A decoy?" asked Sour Sooz.

"Perhaps, but what the hell do we do now?"

I stood up and checked my PPG and my Kevlar before taking my goggles out of my pocket.

"I'll go."

Fourteen

"You can't," said Jack. "You're only a trainee."

"I'm not going to try to catch it," I snapped. Like I would even try. "I'm just going to track it and keep an eye on it until someone who knows what they're doing can get there. Otherwise it could get away, right?"

Jack nodded reluctantly, and I marched out of the room.

Running was not something I did unless I had to, but this seemed to be one of those occasions. Thank God Evie had been making me do all those drills. At least I managed something between a trot and a run up Eastcheap, pulling my goggles on as I went, and not even slowing as I found the puddle of bright that marked the Morph's entry point. Through the clearer top half of the goggles I could see that the slime had already dried away and had left no mark on the street.

The trail took me down Fish Street, then under the King William Street bridge and onto Upper Thames Street. There were more people here, most huddled up against walls or in doorways, looking shocked or angry. The few that were on the street melted away in front of me, and one or two of the more helpful citizens pointed along the road in the direction the Morph had travelled. I even heard a shout of encouragement.

The trail went under something that looked like it might be a railway station, then it ducked down towards the river, twisting and turning through one narrow alley after another. I jogged along as quickly as I could, but my breath burned in my chest and my throat closed up. Endurance was not my strong point.

The Morph trail turned south again and headed for the river, which made me worry. I heard someone say it would head for the water, and it sounded like that was a bad thing. Maybe they could still run underwater, or they changed into a fish, or something. The silver trail led up to the end of the road, then disappeared. I slowed down, trying to catch my breath as I walked, expecting to look over the edge and see the river.

Only there was no water. It was low tide, and what I saw was a short flight of stone steps that led down to the riverbank. The smell was disgusting, and I threw up a little into my mouth before I got myself under control. I spat unpleasantly, then looked down the steps and along the bank. Everything was a mess. The steps were coated in damp algae that looked as slippery as Morph slime, and the riverbank was cluttered with discarded boxes, half-filled sacks and anonymous humps I really didn't want to know anything more about. All coated with a thick layer of river sludge.

I scanned back and forth, through both halves of the goggle lenses, searching any kind of trail. There wasn't so much as a trace. I could see it down the steps, but it got fainter the farther it went into the silt. I stamped my foot in frustration and punched my fists against my thighs. So close, and now I was going to be a joke. Nobody would take me seriously after this; the wannabe warrior who lost her first Morph.

I pulled my goggles away from my eyes and let them dangle around my neck. I had to blink a few times before my vision came back into focus. Losing the split-view of the goggles made my eyes water as they adjusted—well, that was what I told myself—and I wondered if I should head back to the Tower. I could drop off my kit before I jumped home for the last time. I took one more look around as I turned and froze in the middle of taking the first step.

There was a groove in the sludge. The side of my mouth hitched up into a lop-sided grin. The groove was shallow, and only six inches wide, but it clearly moved away from the steps and headed west along the riverbank. It was hardly noticeable when I looked right at it, but from the corner of my eye... I picked my way down the steps and groaned as my boots sank two inches deep into the sludge.

When the groove faded out, I was standing close to a slipway. I put the goggles back on, then punched the air and muttered "Yessss" as a silver trail sprang to life in front of me. Careful steps up the slipway, then I followed the trail as it turned through a set of open gates. They were wooden, with patches of peeling paint and a sign above that said "Queenshithe Wharf.".

I hesitated at the entrance. The Morph might be trapped in there. Farther up the street there seemed to be a commotion going on, but the trail led into the wharf. A moment later, a Grenlik ran through the gates, eyes wide, pushing past me and looking anxiously over his shoulder. He pointed an unsteady finger back towards the gates and said, "It's in there" as he hurried off to join his companions at the end of the street.

I looked into the yard. Opposite me was what seemed to be a block of offices and to my right, a larger structure with several barn-sized doors. From the back, I guessed the buildings on either side of the gate might be the same. In the yard were piles of crates, laid out in a haphazard arrangement that rose higher than my head.

This had "trap" written all over it. I could see the trail going through the gate, then turning left before and disappearing from view. The sensible thing to do was to stand at the gate and wait for help. I'd tracked it this far, and I couldn't see how it could get out. That was as much as anyone could ask of me.

Except I wasn't sure. I couldn't see the whole yard. If there was another gate on the other side, I'd look exceptionally stupid for not checking.

I reached down and snapped the loop off the PPG's holster before drawing it and giving it a quick visual check. The charge jewel said it was full, so I flicked off the safety and edged into the yard.

Part of me wanted to take the goggles off, to see everything I could with nothing in the way, and if I could have guaranteed the Morph would stay in monster shape, I would have taken the chance. But for all I knew, it could be one of the larger crates. Nobody had told me what a Morph could or couldn't change into. The only way I knew what I was looking at was if a trail of silver led to it.

The wall to my left looked clean; no boxes, only a blank wall with one double door. I put my back to it and crabbed towards the river. I was safe on two sides; one I had my back against and the other taken up by water; a proper quay with mooring bollards and lifting engines, but no ships.

My eyes flickered back and forth across the yard, scanning for any sign of movement. The silver trail went halfway along the front of the wharf, then turned north and disappeared amongst the piles of goods. Exactly what I had hoped wouldn't happen.

I still couldn't see if there was a gate on the other side of the yard, but if I went into the jumbled merchandise, the Morph could sneak out when I wasn't looking. I crept back to the gate and tried my luck along the other wall. There were more things scattered about here, but no silver trail, so I figured none of them could be the Morph. And I had a good view of the gate I came through in case the Morph made a run for it. Three safe sides.

I slid along the north wall, trying to look in three directions at once and determined to stop as soon as I could see if there was another exit. Out of sight, on the west side of the yard, something fell to the ground with a crash and I heard movement. Was something making a break for it through some door I hadn't seen yet? I ran along the rest of the wall. As I cleared the edge of the stacks in the middle of the yard, I saw there was no gate and that someone had knocked a pile of boxes over. There was no trail of silver, and my heart sank. It had duped me, drawn me out of position. The Morph was probably already halfway up the street. My shoulders sagged. I didn't have the breath, or the will, left to chase after it. I put the PPG in its holster and sighed before I turned back towards the gate.

The stack of boxes nearest me exploded, pelting me with wood and apples. I felt the Kevlar flash warm against my chest as it deflected the shrapnel, but the sheer volume of material knocked me off my feet and pushed me back against the wall. A moment later, the next stack along rippled and flowed into the reptilian shape of an attacking Morph.

I was already moving, rolling to my right over and over until I heard the thump of the Morph's tongue strike somewhere behind me. Now I knew I had a second or two before it could strike again. My next roll brought me to my feet, and I dived into the piles of boxes the Morph had come from. I would use its own trick against it. A shower of splinters flew at me from the Morph's next punch, but the Kevlar deflected them. They seemed to get a lot closer, though. I jinked right, then left, then right again. The river was ahead of me now. I clawed the PPG out of its holster as I dodged.

Behind me, I heard the Morph barging through the piles of goods, throwing things aside in its eagerness. It wanted me, perhaps out of the way before it tried to escape, or perhaps just for spite. I hesitated for a second, then gambled. I shoved at the stack nearest to me, collapsing it back towards all the other produce, then I broke for the east wall, turning so I was running backwards. The wall thumped me so hard I almost winded myself, just as the Morph broke free from the mess in the middle of the yard. The PPG was ready in my hands, and it seemed to track the target on its own. My finger tapped the trigger three times, sending out a spread of glittering purple that crossed every line the Morph could take like a submarine firing torpedoes. Two hit the Morph at the same time, and it sank to the ground as a pool of gel.

I drew in a deep breath, my jaw clenched so hard it hurt, and my heartbeat hammering in my ears as I tried to sort out everything that was whirling around in my head. Booted feet ran towards me, and I turned my head in time to see two Warriors run through the gate, PPGs raised and ready. They skidded to a halt when they saw me. One was, to my surprise, Evie. Both grew wide grins on their faces. The one I didn't know, a bulky boy with a blond fuzz-cut, walked up to me with his hand out.

"First kill?" he asked.

"Second," shouted Evie.

"First *official* kill," I said, taking the boy's hand and letting him pull me up. He shook it before he let go.

"Whatever," he said, chuckling. "Welcome to the most exclusive club in the world."

He waved and walked away. Evie stepped forward once he had left. She looked uncertain, shifting her weight from one foot to the other, bottom lip caught between her teeth. "That was pretty stupid."

I nodded but couldn't wipe the grin off my face. "It's not like I meant to. I was only going to follow it."

"Even got that wrong," Evie was grinning too, now, and there was no malice in her words. She half raised her arms, looking shy and awkward, and I stepped forward into the hug. It was brief, but intense, and we turned and walked towards the gate. "How are you feeling?"

"OK. Buzzing. Scared. Wonderful. Everything's unreal."

"Want me to say you're tired?"

"Why?"

Evie nudged my arm and pointed with her chin. Halfway up the street was a tall figure with wild, unruly hair and a look of near panic on his face. As soon as he saw them, Jack started forward, then stopped, then started walking again.

"Thanks, but I think I'm OK."

Evie held out her hand, and I didn't understand. "Your PPG," said Evie. "You can't jump home if you're carrying. I'll take it back to the Tower for you."

I gave her a lopsided grin as I handed my weapon over. Evie peeled away with a wave, disappearing into the crowd. Claire could hear her telling everybody that the fun was over and they should find something else to look at.

"I was really worried about you," Jack said. "I shouldn't have let you go."

"Couldn't have stopped me."

He looked down at her. "Probably not. How are you feeling?"

I thought for a moment. "Hungry. Hungry enough to eat a horse."

"Around here, you might wish you were," said Jack, pulling a wry face. "My treat?"

I looped my arm through his. "Absolutely."

Fifteen

I sat in the lounge with my parents, watching the evening news as I ate vegetarian spagbol from the plate on my lap. I wasn't paying attention to the TV until the words "Evelyn Jones" seared into my mind. Rich red sauce sloshed towards the edge of the plate as I lunged for the remote. My parents made questioning noises as I TIVO'd the news item back to the beginning, then I waved at them to be quiet as I hit "play".

"Police are tonight looking for a college girl from Harland," said the news anchor. A grainy photo that didn't look like Evie, yet was still clearly her, flicked up behind the anonymous presenter. "Evelyn Jones has not been seen for three days. Our reporter, Martin Ellis, spoke to her guardian."

The picture cut away to a woman sitting in an office. She looked about the same age as my mum, but more harassed. Her hair frizzed and she needed to change the theme of her makeup. The worry in her eyes was genuine and sharp. Off camera, a male voice asked questions.

"I understand Evelyn has been living in care for some years. Does she have a history of running away?"

"No, she—"

"Does she have a reputation for being in trouble with the police? Would that be why she has gone missing?"

"Evie has no record of involvement with the police."

"Is this gang related, Mrs Nixon? Or drugs?" the eagerness in the reporter's voice to associate Evie with something ugly made me feel sick with anger. Seemed he pushed the carer's buttons too.

"Evie has never gone missing before," she said. Her name came to me just before the caption popped up: Meg Nixon. When the idiot reporter tried to interrupt her again, she drove right over him. "She has an outstanding record and is working hard to finish a college course. An absence of this duration is totally out of character."

The camera cut away to a follow-up shot of a male reporter with bouffant hair and a dated collar. "There we have it. A vulnerable young woman, apparently missing under mysterious circumstance, desperately sought by police. Back to you in the studio."

I pressed the button that let the PVR return to real-time, then sat back on the sofa, dinner forgotten. Evie had missed our last appointment, which had been on Wednesday. I had gone to the library again on the Thursday and Friday, but still no Evie. Today was Sunday, and perhaps now I had the 'why'—or at least part of it.

"Why the big frown, squirt?" asked her father. "You look like you saw a ghost."

"Nothing. I mean, I thought I recognised the girl in the news, but I don't know the name. Made me feel spooky, though." I stood up and turned to my mum. "Mind if I don't finish this? It's nice, but I don't feel hungry anymore."

"Of course not, sweetie," she said, reaching out and rubbing my hip, which was the only bit of me she could reach. "You can snack later if you change your mind."

I dumped the plate in the kitchen and went up to my room. What should I do? I couldn't go to the police. What could I say? Nor did I have any way to contact Evie. I asked, twice, for her mobile number, but Evie always told me she didn't believe in mobiles. And I still couldn't jump in on her own.

It was two weeks since I had made my second kill. Evie had turned up every time she said she would, but we split up three or four hours into each trip. She left me to find my own amusements and my own way out. Most of my free time I spent with Jack, while Evie was increasingly distant, with her mind on something else.

I even asked if Evie was getting bored with training me, or if I wasn't making enough progress. She was apologetic, saying she was really busy at the moment and not to worry because they had another two months before I would get her final assessment. Except it wasn't. I was down to five weeks.

The missed appointments and this news item added up to something uncomfortable, and I couldn't shift a deep belief that the police were looking in the wrong place. What I could do about it was a different problem. There was nobody I could contact to jump me into Underland. My closest option was to try to get one of the geek squad at school to jump me in, but the shame would be unbearable and the chance that anyone would actually help me zero.

I tried to jump to the spot in front of my locker over and over, and every failure left me more stressed. Mum took to checking my temperature with her hand on my forehead, and offering infusions of St John's Wort and asking if I was feeling depressed about going back to school. Dad even offered a stock yet totally heartfelt 'you know you can talk to me about anything, don't you?'. I wished I could tell them. Wished I could tell somebody. Wished I could tell Jack. At least he would believe me.

Why had I never swapped mobile numbers with him? I trawled for him in all the go-to social media places, but his name was too common and there was never a picture that looked enough like him to take a chance on. When I finally admitted defeat, the size of the sigh and the wave of sadness that washed over me was a complete surprise.

And that was what gave me the idea. What if jumping wasn't about concentration? What if it was about the connection you had with wherever you were trying to get? I put on my Warrior gear. My jaw tightened up and the emo-deep funk that had collected around me blew away like smog. I was Warrior Stone, with two kills to my name before I was out of training and I could do this. In the middle of my bedroom, I tried to visualise the Observer post where Jack worked. I built it, focused on it, let it build around me and seep into me, and turned.

Nothing happened, but a moment later I realised that wasn't true. I had felt something, like the expectation that always preceded a jump. So was I on the right track, but maybe not quite in the right place? Jack told me that Runners trained for months before they were trusted to jump on their own, building up the image of the jump room until it was burned into their minds, and that made me feel a little better if no less frustrated. So what was sharper in my mind than Jack's office? A grin crept over my face as I let a new image build in my thoughts. I carefully edited out any time cues, and let it suffuse through me before I applied a twist and...

There were angry mutters from a small crowd around me, and a female Hrund was being helped from the floor where, presumably, the force of my arrival had knocked her. I almost went to help before I realised that would make the situation worse. Instead, I bowed deeply. "My profound apologies, Sa. This is an emergency."

The Hrund gave me a displeased look, but then offered a curt nod of acknowledgement. I hurried away into the underground station. At the far end of the platform, I did a little two-step dance back and forth as I waited for a train. When it came in,

I jumped into the front carriage and jabbed the Warrior-only button until the door closed.

The ride, like the wait, seemed to last forever. When the doors did finally hiss open, I twisted through them as quickly as I could and was running into the building before I heard the train pull away.

And then I was standing in the main corridor of the SFU offices, realising that I didn't have a clue what to do next. The locker room seemed an unlikely place to find anything useful, but I knew my way to that best. As usual, there was nobody else there, which was a quirk I had never understood. I walked up to Evie's locker. Somebody had stuck a yellow label next to the lock. The label had no words on it, and there was a thin film of dust on top of the handle. Nobody had opened it in days. I looked closer and saw somebody had picked off two of Evie's kill-markers.

A hot flash of fury flickered over me. Something was very much not right.

It took me a while to find the stores. I had only been there once, but other than the posh office and the target range, it was the only other place I knew in the headquarters. I pushed through the correct door. All three gates were closed, and there was an oppressive silence hanging over the empty room. I was about to walk out when I noticed a tiny silver bell hanging from a piece of string tied to one railing. I walked up to it and gave it a gentle shake.

There was a distant muttering. I couldn't tell if it was one voice or several, but footsteps scuffled towards me from somewhere off to the left. I wished they would hurry, and as I drew breath to call out a Grenlik walked from behind a line of shelving. Only it wasn't who I expected.

"What is this?" the Grenlik complained. "Don't you people understand break times?"

"Sorry, there was nothing on the door."

"What do you want? Where is your requisition chit? I don't have all day to waste while you dither."

I tried to figure out a polite way to ask, then gave up. "Look, I'm sorry if this offends anybody, and I know about the name thing and all that, but I need to speak to Krosset, and I need to speak to him now. Please. It's really urgent."

The Grenlik glowered at me, and one side of its mouth lifted in either a sneer or a snarl, but it turned and wandered back into the shelving. I hoped it wasn't ignoring me and going back to its lunch. The shuffling paused for a moment, then got louder again, only this time the gait was heavier. After what felt like an eternity, Krosset stood at the middle gate and glared at her. "I assume there is an excellent reason for this?" He sounded offended.

"I know I just busted about ten rules of proper behaviour, but I don't know everything yet, and I don't think I have time to find out. So can we please just leave it that I'm a bad person who hopes to do better? I needed to speak to you. Evie has gone missing and I don't know who to talk to about it. I know it's not you, I only know you, so you were the only place I could start." I realised I was babbling and forced myself to shut up, then looked hopefully at the Grenlik.

Krosset lost his angry expression, which changed to something more understanding. "It happens to all of you in time," he said. "You should start by talking to Human Resources. Second floor, room 209. Next door to Personnel."

"Thank you," I said, already halfway out of the room.

In the second-floor office, only one of the three desks was occupied, and the Sathaari was not pleased at being distracted from the small meal in front of him.

"Please, it's so important," I begged, and he dabbed at the corners of his perfectly clean mouth with a napkin, before draping it over his food as though he expected me to spray spit over it.

"Very well," he said with a theatrical sigh. "What seems to be the problem?"

"Evie, I mean Warrior Jones, has been reported missing."

"Yes." He drawled in a "tell me something I didn't know" voice, which sucked the wind from my sails. I did an impression of a stranded fish.

"You know?"

"I know that Warrior Jones has not reported for duty for a week. She did not advise us in advance of any planned absence. Given Jones' age, it was only a matter of time before she became unable to jump into Underland, and we assume this time has arrived."

"No. You don't understand. Evie isn't in the Over. She's down here. She must be. They've reported her missing to the police."

"We have no evidence of that. Without evidence, we must assume that Jones it still in the Over. Any issues or difficulties she may experience there are beyond our jurisdiction. Now, if you wouldn't mind?" He waved a hand across his napkin-covered plate and raised his eyebrows as if questioning my continued presence in his office. I tried to speak, twice, but both times nothing came to me that had any chance of swaying the bureaucrat's mind, so I turned and left, closing the door gently behind me.

What could I do now? I knew so little about the non-physical side of the SFU, and apart from Evie and Krosset, I didn't know anybody else in the whole of Underland. Apart from Jack. I reached into my pocket for my communicator, pressed the blue gem to open a call, and spoke Jack's name. When he answered, it still surprised me how clear the voices were from the little box.

"Hi. Where have you been?"

"Long story. I need to talk to you."

"Sure, I'm off duty in about three hours."

"No, sooner."

"Okay," his tone shifted to something placating, reacting to the tension in my voice. "I can sneak out for fifteen minutes. Perhaps a half hour."

I fumed. "That'll have to do."

"Where?"

I tried to think of somewhere close they both knew.

"The squash parlour on Harp Lane?"

"I know it. be there as soon as I can."

I closed the connection and set off.

It was only after I ordered a pitcher of squash I realised I had nothing to pay with, and hoped Jack wouldn't mind. As a Warrior I got paid, as a trainee I got nothing. I had finished my glass and was considering starting on his by the time he showed up. He took a seat next to me, ignored the squash, and got right to the point.

"What's the panic?"

I told him about the missing person report, and what the Sathaari in H.R. had said. Jack sat back and looked thoughtful.

"I don't understand why you're so worried. If she is missing in the Over, then there's nothing you can do."

"But she isn't. She's here. I know she is."

"Know? How?"

My lips made a tight, angry line. This was not going how I had expected. He was supposed to be my friend, to believe me. "All right, I don't 'know' know, but she wouldn't get herself in any trouble in the Over. She's too smart for that and everything in her life revolved around Underland."

"How long have you known her?" asked Jack, his tone like a grown-up about to make a point.

I knew where he was trying to go. "Six months," I said.

"More like two, if you take out the gaps. And you only know what she told you. You know everybody thinks she's borderline crazy, don't you?" I glared at him, and Jack had the grace to go red. It had been an unfair comment. "I'm just saying you might not know her as well as you think."

"And it sounds to me like you've made no effort at all. To know her, I mean."

Jack shrugged. "Maybe, but she never went out of her way to be sociable. All she ever wanted to do was go around bursting Morphs."

I scowled at him some more, then looked away. "Whatever. I still think she is here, and she could need help."

Jack sat back in his chair and picked up his squash. The Hrund chose that exact moment to come out and place the bill on the table. I couldn't look at him, and eventually Jack chuckled and threw a couple of coins into the bowl placed over the bill, to stop it fluttering away.

"This is that important to you?"

I nodded and Jack sighed. "I don't know what to suggest. Everything that goes anywhere goes through Aslnaff."

I felt my shoulders droop and pushed myself up from the chair. Jack rose too. "I'm sorry about the squashes," I said, waving a hand at the table. "I'll pay you back someday."

"Forget it." Jack sounded like he was trying to make light, then he leaned sideways and gave her an awkward, quick hug.

I tensed up, surprised by the contact. Jack froze, then jerked his arms away.

"Sorry, I..."

"Look, it..."

We spoke together, and both tailed off. Jack waved his hand to show he was waiting for me. "It's nothing personal," I said, with my eyes on the floor. "I suppose I'm edgy."

Jack nodded and walked out of the parlour. "Got to get back. Let me know how you get on." He didn't turn but threw a wave over his shoulder.

I watched him go, surprised by how angry I was. It took some thought to realise that I was madder at me than at Jack. That was not how it had been supposed to happen. We were supposed to be standing side by side watching trains from a bridge, or alone in a watch tower. And I wasn't supposed to go spiky and brush him off. I gave him time to turn the corner at the end of the street before I set off in the same direction.

SIXTEEN

The next morning, I jumped in right in front of my locker, which surprised the heck out of me. An envelope had been stuck to the door. I peeled it off, but before I could open it, I saw underneath the envelope somebody had stuck two slightly second-hand kill-stickers to my door. I got a lump in my throat as I ran my fingers across them.

A deep breath later, I opened the envelope, hoping it was a note from Evie. As soon as I saw the formal-looking cream paper, I knew it wasn't. It was addressed to "Trainee Stone".

"You are required to present yourself to the Administrator's office at your earliest convenience, or to arrange an appointment to do so, before you engage in any further training or operational activities for the SFU."

It had the administrator's name at the bottom, with an illegible scrawl above it. I'd read enough military sci fi to know that 'earliest convenience' meant 'now', so I made my way up to the administrative floor. The Hrund kept her face neutral, but it was obvious that I was expected, and equally obvious that the Hrund knew why.

So did I. I had been asking questions and rubbing people up the wrong way. I had gone from Post to Post asking if anybody knew anything about Evie's movements or activities. I had even been to the Central Police Station, right here in the same compound as the SFU building. Someone had told me I could speak directly to the Station Commander if a member of the SFU was being abused, but the chat had escalated into a row, and I jumped out in the middle of it. Which was probably rude.

Aslnaff kept me waiting, which again was no surprise. He was trying to show me how unimportant I was. Hadn't worked last time, and it wasn't going to work now, but he was making me so angry by the time I was told to go through my jaw was clenched and I pulled the door open so hard I felt I might rip it off its hinges.

I walked up to the desk and stood in front of it. Aslnaff didn't look up, but shuffled papers back and forth on his desk and pretended to peruse one or two. This again? It pushed me past being polite.

"You asked to see me, Administrator," I said, voice strong and choosing my words deliberately.

Aslnaff's head shot up. "I *sent* for you, trainee. I sent for you because I will not tolerate any more of this foolishness about Warrior Jones. If Jones has experienced some difficulty in the Over, that is regrettable but beyond our jurisdiction and area of responsibility. If, as is far more likely given her age, Jones simply cannot enter Underland anymore—well, it is unfortunate and perhaps you would pass on our appreciation for her efforts when you next see her. But Jones is not in Underland, in difficulty or otherwise, and I will not have you embarrassing me, or the rest of the SFU, with any further nonsense such as the regrettable incident with the Station Commander. I have no idea how you came by this arcane precedent, but whoever told you about it counselled you poorly."

My heart pounded and my breaths got deeper during Aslnaff's oration. I felt my lips compressed into a hard, thin line, and my breath whistled through my nose. I was a second away from shouting a defiant argument back at him, but at the last second, I bit my tongue. Aslnaff was trying to push me into an outburst. Then he could he use that to throw me out. I let the breath out, made an effort to relax, and tried again.

"Sorry, Administrator. I'm only trying to act in the best interests of a fellow Warrior, and the SFU."

Aslnaff blinked hard and looked surprised, and I smothered a smile. I'd confused him. "Yes, well," he blustered. "Laudable, I am sure, but—"

"Please, Ser." The interruption earned me a glare that made Aslnaff look like he was peering at an unsightly bug on the end of his nose. "I understand that maybe nothing official can be done, but what about in my spare time? I would like to be allowed to look for Ev—Warrior Jones, or to see if I can find out anything about where she was last seen."

Aslnaff sputtered for a moment. "Absolutely not. The only reason any human has to be in Underland is performing their SFU duties. This is not some recreational resource for dilettante teenagers. Your actions could bring shame to the department. It is essential that you act within departmental policy at all times, and I fear that Jones neglected this part of your training."

He stopped and took a long, hissing breath through his nose as he pointedly rolled his shoulders. One hand rose to smooth at what was left of his hair, then rejoined its twin, interleaved on the desk. His voice was much calmer when he continued. "I must say that I had grave doubts regarding Jones' somewhat grandiose plans for late-entry Warriors, and it would seem my concerns have been vindicated. However, you have made a contribution, and you obviously have some aptitude. Therefore, I am reassigning you to the grade of Junior Observer. You will be assigned duty station and rotation accordingly, and it will be the responsibility of your assigned Senior Observer to ensure you are properly trained in the basics. Have to learn to walk before we can fly, eh?"

Aslnaff delivered this in a way that made him come over like a creepy uncle, or a teacher trying to be 'cool', and I had to smother a laugh. I wasn't about to give in. If it had been anyone other than Evie, I probably would have. For now, I might need the SFU, and if this was the only way to keep that, then I had to bow down and take it. It still tasted very bitter.

"OK," was the best I could manage without saying something I shouldn't. Again, the look of surprise on Aslnaff's face was some reward, even though this time it had a tinge of suspicion.

"Very well. Inform stores of your change of status and they will arrange for your equipment transfer. You can turn in your Mk.22 and your goggles immediately."

I hadn't thought of that, and I felt a little stupid. It was going to be much more dangerous moving around in Underland without my Warrior's equipment. Still, I nodded to Aslnaff, who was already looking down at the paperwork he had been pretending to study when I came in. He flicked his fingers to dismiss at me. Biting the inside of my cheek, I turned and left the room as I tried to figure out how I was going to get around Aslnaff.

Seventeen

Krosset stood at the window when I shuffled into the Stores. Someone I didn't know was being served, so I hung back until they were done, exchanging a polite nod as they left. Krosset was giving me a strange look as I walked up to the counter, carrying my PPG and my goggles.

"You heard?" I said.

Krosset nodded. "More than you might think." He took my gun and my goggles and handed me a chit to say I had returned them. I smiled sadly and turned away, but Krosset called me back.

"One moment, Warrior."

It surprised me how good it made me feel to be called that. I turned back and raised my eyebrows at the Grenlik, but he was mulling something over that left him reluctant to speak. I waited. He usually had something worthwhile to say.

"Warrior Jones has a number on the back of her Kevlar," he said, and I thought the comment a bit random. "It's the inverse of yours, which is a total coincidence."

"I suppose it is," I said, trying to keep the bemusement off my face and out of my voice.

"People are often unimaginative with the security codes on their lockers," he added. "They are lazy, and predictable."

"Really?" I looked up at the ceiling for a moment. I set my locker code to the same as the number on the back of my amulet.

Krosset nodded. "Oh, they are. And very busy we are, too. You'll have to wait at least a week for us to reclaim the outstanding equipment from your locker. Administration will have to wait even longer for Warrior Jones' effects. She has to be out of contact for another three weeks before we can even raise the paperwork to put her things back into storage." He started shaking his head instead. "Things can move so slowly sometimes."

He pulled the shutter down and turned away, carrying off my weapon and my goggles, and waving over his shoulder. I looked at his receding back and tried to stop the grin spreading over my lips. I still had things to do inside the building. People would pay me too much attention if I didn't look miserable.

For the first time, and probably because I wanted it quiet, the locker room was busy. There were four observers in various aisles, and a conversation I had heard from outside the door—shouted from row to row—fell silent as I entered. Picking a bench as far away from everybody else as I could, I sat with my head hanging, trying to look like I just wanted to be left alone. The Observers drifted towards each other, huddled into a knot, and started whispering in scandalised tones as they migrated out into the corridor.

I waited until I heard the door clunk shut into its frame, then checked the rest of the room. When I was sure I was alone, I stepped over to Evie's locker and used my code, reversed. For a moment, I thought Krosset had made a mistake. The door wouldn't open. I gave it another experimental yank and realised it was sticking at the top. I pulled harder, with an extra tug downward, and the door popped open. Then I groaned. There was a colossal mess of stuff everywhere but—and this was such a big but—no duster coat and no PPG in the clip at the back. Evie was still in Underland.

There was too much to carry, but I had no time to sort through it all now. I ran over to my locker and jerked it open. I left a shoulder bag inside a week ago and had forgotten to take it home. It was strong, made of black canvas, and could carry most of Evie's stuff. I slammed my door, in case someone jumped in and hit themselves on it, and ran back to Evie's locker, cramming the bag with anything that didn't look like abandoned food, spare clothes, or litter. When I reached the bottom of the pile and pulled aside something that looked like it might have been an item of clothing, I gasped and stepped back.

Lying on the locker floor was a battered holster, and inside was a PPG.

I couldn't wear it. I was supposed to be nothing more than an observer now. On the other hand, I wasn't going to ignore such a handout. I stuffed it into the bag, packing other things around it to make the shape less obvious, then shut the door and walked out of the locker room.

There was nobody in the private underground station, so I took a train to Commercial Road. Cotton Street I found easily enough, but all the little shops looked the same, even though I walked all the way along the street and peered at the front of each arch. Many I could ignore; they were open, and either had display windows or goods out on the street. I could also eliminate anything too close to either end of the road because I remembered walking quite a way before Evie had hammered on a door. By the time I had finished my Sherlock Holmes act, I had four arches that seemed to offer the best chance of finding Tolks.

I noticed someone staring at me. Several someones. I was drawing attention to herself. Walking up and down the street, then standing and staring across the bustling thoroughfare, was not a particularly innocent action. Would the SFU have spies out here? Would they be looking for me? My eyes tracked upwards, looking for any Observation towers, though a moment later I remembered there weren't any for a mile. I gritted my teeth and looked across the road; Time to get on with it, or get out of there and try again later—if there was a later.

I went up to the first alcove and hammered on the door. The Grenlik in the store to my left leaned out through his door and scowled at me as he hooked the bottom of his shutter and pulled it down. I made a face at the grating and hammered again. There was no answer.

I moved on to the next alcove. This one had no shutter, but there was no shop front either and the door, when I tried it, was locked. I knocked loudly and was sure I saw a flicker of movement through the translucent pane in the window. I knocked again, trying to make it sound as though I wasn't going to take no for an answer. A policeman's knock. I put my ear to the door. Scuffing footsteps drew closer, and I jerked away as rusty bolts scraped. The door opened a few inches, held in place by a chain, and a suspicious face peered out of the gap.

That was when I realised I didn't know what to say. Grenlix were pathologically suspicious and were so hung up about names that I couldn't think how I could ask for him without naming him. "Grenlik," I said and bowed my head, playing for time. The face cut me no slack.

"What?"

"I seek a Grenlik who works on this street," I began, speaking slowly as I tried to weave the question. "He works with others to repair things."

"There are three," said the face, and the door started to close. I jammed most of my foot into the gap, then had a flashback to my first day on the job. In the ballet pumps I wore then, the door would have crushed my foot.

"The one I want works with others, very near here."

"I don't know him," said the face, and slammed harder the door on my foot. "Go away."

I dropped my voice and tried to make it a bit menacing. "I know his name, Grenlik, and I'm sure you do, too. Apart from messing with a Warrior, do you want me to tell him I had to stand out in the middle of the street shouting his name because you wouldn't tell me which shop was his?"

The face at the door looked a little less certain of itself, but no less hostile. It growled, spat at the floor next to my foot, before a bony finger pointed to my right. "Four doors down, human." She spat the last word out, an unveiled insult.

I held eye contact as I pulled my foot back and made no attempt to offer her thanks. The door slammed shut, and I flipped my middle finger at it before moving down the street. When I reached Tolks' door, it did seem familiar now I knew it was the right one, and I hammered on it.

"Closed!"

The voice was familiar, too, and I felt a flush of relief as I hammered again.

"It's Warrior Stone," I said, loudly but not shouting.

"Still closed."

"Don't make me yell your name out here," I replied, more quietly. It sounded like Tolks was on the other side of the door, and I didn't want to make the confrontation any more public than it had to be. That would just make things harder later. "And don't make me say how much help Warrior Jones said you were."

There was the sound of bolts being pulled back and the door creaked ajar. I eased it open wide enough to slip through, then closed it behind me. I turned, raising my hand to slide one of the bolts back into place, but hesitated. Did I want to be locked in here? If things got nasty, could I get out quickly? I dropped my hand to the smallest bolt and pushed it home. Enough to keep out casual visitors, but I should be able to pull the door open despite it if I had to. I turned into the room and made my way across the gloomy outer shop, towards the door to the space at the back.

Tolks stood in the middle of the workshop, arms crossed in front of him and feet planted at shoulder width. He did not look happy, and the three youngsters sitting at the bench were very careful to make it very obvious they were not paying any attention at all.

"That was not appropriate," said Tolks, glowering. "One does not threaten another with whom names have been exchanged."

I was still thinking on the run, but I was tired, and tired of all this nonsense. "Then you could try answering a knock on the door with something other than "Closed". Give me a break, will you? I've only been here for a few weeks. I need to talk to you and I have nobody to ask about the finer points of Grenlik etiquette."

"Perhaps I was hasty—"

"Yes, you were."

"Hasty in assuming you were a person worthy of sharing names. It seems Warrior Jones still has some way to go with your training."

"And I wouldn't need to do this if I could ask her. Ev... Warrior Jones has gone missing."

"An accident Above? A shame." Tolks was already turning away, and I couldn't decide if he already knew, or had been told what to say. The ground I was walking on suddenly felt like ice, and thin ice at that. I had no friends down here, apart from Jack and Evie, and maybe Krosset. How huge what I was trying to do loomed over me, threatening to topple and crush me. But Evie trusted Tolks, and if Evie trusted him, she would have a good reason. I took the chance. After all, I had no other lead to follow.

"Evie isn't in the Over. Wherever she is, she's down here."

Tolks stopped and turned back. "What makes you say that?"

"Many things. Mostly that loads of her stuff wasn't in her locker."

"Not convincing."

"Her PPG was missing, and her holster, plus her goggles and coat and all the other equipment she took out with her when she was here. Evie wouldn't take anything like that Over. She'd never do anything she could get kicked out for."

Tolks unfolded one arm and stroked his chin with a hand. "Interesting, but still not convincing. There is much that could explain her absence, or the absence of her belongings. Someone could have stolen them."

"Really? Can you imagine what Jones would do to anyone she caught stealing from her?"

A flicker of a smile ghosted around Tolks' lips. "Also true." Again, he turned away, but he moved only so far as to climb onto a stool. His workbench was set apart from the long one used by the others. There was less clutter here, and only a few devices. He flicked a cloth out to cover what he had been working on and waved me towards another stool.

"Can you tell me anything?" I pleaded. "Evie trusted you. Did she tell you anything that might explain where she is?"

Tolks was already shaking his head before I finished talking. "I'm pleased that Warrior Jones trusted me, and it is because she trusted me, I can tell you nothing, even if I knew anything that would be of help to you. What worth would my trust be then?"

"But not even if she's in trouble?"

"I am sure you have the best intentions, but the path to chaos is paved with such. Without being sure that Jones would want, or need, me to share her secrets with you, I cannot help."

Eighteen

My bottom lip pouted like a baby, and I quickly covered the emerging sulk with a frown. "So what am I supposed to do? The SFU says she's forgotten how to jump in, and the police say there isn't any evidence to prove she is still in Underland, so they don't want to know either. Am I supposed to forget about it and go home? Leave her?"

Tolks' eyebrows had clicked out sideways. "So, it might seem, many want you to think."

"Pardon?"

"Does it not strike you as odd that nobody is prepared to consider even the possibility that Warrior Jones might be in Underland?" Tolks shook his head. "I fear this pot is too deep for me to stir, and I wonder if you are wise to do so." He rubbed at his nose. "I can offer you this. If Jones has left such titbits as will lead you on to more, then that is her concern and I betray no confidences. Jones has a room, here in Underland. It is on an outside wall of Hive Straknat, which you will find at the corner of Felton Street and Harvey Street. Many know this, so I betray no confidence. Enter through the door at that corner. Ask for "the Grenlik Hivemaster" but accept a subordinate. That is all I can offer you."

It was less than I hoped to get out of him, but it was something. I hoped Evie's friendship would count for more, and that the Grenlik would summon a posse of streetwise helpers and start scouring the city for clues. What he had offered me was better than nothing, though. I slid off the stool and made my way to the front of the shop, the only other sound the muffled shuffle of Tolks' feet behind me. At the door, I turned. "What is the right way to ask for you?" I asked.

Tolks' wiry eyebrows rose a fraction, and the corner of his mouth quirked upwards for a second. "Without a Warrior's uniform often works better."

I nodded and bowed. Tolks returned the bow with equal gravity. "Good luck, Warrior Stone." I opened the door, walked outside, and heard it close gently behind me.

Now all I had to do was find Felton Street or Harvey Street. I reached into my pocket and pulled out my communicator. Jack would know. I held it to my mouth but didn't speak. Jack would want to know why, and if I didn't tell him, I would probably find him sitting at the corner waiting for me. I wanted to tell myself I didn't want to get him into any trouble. I also wanted to believe he wouldn't tell anybody where I was, or push me to find out what I was doing. But, to my horror, I couldn't. Had things really got so bad I couldn't even trust Jack? Damn Tolks and his Grenlik paranoia. Feeling very alone, I put the communicator back in my pocket.

As I walked back to the underground station, I kept my eyes open for a constable. Evie told me once they were like a walking street map. When I found one, he was an Angel, walking along the opposite side of the street towards me. I crossed the road, dodging between a cart being pulled by a steam 'donkey' and an omnibus. "Excuse me." The Angel walked straight past without even looking at me and, without thinking, I grabbed his arm and called, "Hey."

A metallic, electric jolt made my hand and arm jerk. The Angel twisted away with a snarl in his own language, and as he turned back to me, his hand was already drawing his nightstick from a loop on his belt. I stepped back, my hands open and raised, horrified by what I'd just done.

"Idiot! Are you stupid? Don't you care how your foul touch injures others?"

There was no good answer to that question, and I was in the wrong.

"I'm really sorry. I forgot."

"Forgot? A warrior?"

If I said I was only a trainee, I would draw attention to myself I didn't want. But all Angels were bullies at heart, and the only way to deal with a bully was to confront them. "You walked right past me. You want to talk to me about manners?" I made a point of looking at the constable's shoulders, as if trying to see his official number. He was too tall, and the Angel stood up straighter when he realised it. "What did you want?"

"Directions, please, to Felton St."

"I know no such place," said the Angel, and he turned away. I stood my ground and cleared my throat, and he stopped. "What? What would you have me say?"

"You're a constable. You have no idea?"

He pulled an angry face. "And I care less. Take the underground west, perhaps to Broad Street. Ask again there."

This time, he walked off without another glance. I let him go. All the other police I met with had at least been professional, if not courteous. But then, this was the first Angel I'd met ever, and I wondered if they were all so rude. It didn't seem worth wasting any more time on, so I walked down to the trains and did what he suggested.

A more public-spirited policeman at Broad Street gave me better directions, and I left the underground at a station called Arlington Square. Felton St was a short walk away, on the south side of Branch Bridge. The outward appearance of Hive Straknat was almost a copy of where Tolks lived, with even more shops around the edges. Here, though, more people milled around, and the shops had not just Grenlik customers, but Hrund and Sithaari, too. As I walked along the side of the building, I looked up at the small, forbidding windows ranked along the wall above me and wondered if Evie's room was behind one of them. I hoped so. There was something uncomfortable about the idea of going too deep inside the hive or, worse, under it.

At the end of Felton St, on the corner of the building, was a doorway, set back into the angle of the corner. The strong double doors had heavy hinges and iron banding riveted across them. One side was open and there was a steady stream of Grenlix in and out. To my surprise, I saw a Hrund stroll in, and an Angel stepped out, looking nervously back and forth before disappearing into the crowd. Apparently, it wasn't only the shops that were more cosmopolitan.

As I waited for a gap in the traffic, I heard a bell chime above me. I looked up, then took a step back and looked again. Above the door was a tower, and in the tower was a clock face. The clock had only an hour hand, but the face was elegant, even beautiful. But then I saw a space in the flow of bodies, and I hurried through the door. Inside there was another pair of doors, like an airlock. These were also open and led into a hall. It stretched the height of the building, with balconies around each floor above. Hrund stood guard at each arched exit and at the stairwells, one on either side of the hall. The floor was a heavy grey stone that looked rough and gritty and dark wood panelled the walls. Although there were windows along two walls of each balcony, the hall was gloomy, and the magic-fed lights that dotted the walls only seemed to make the shadows deeper.

A window set into one of the wooden walls looked like it might be an enquiry desk. There was a narrow shelf in front of it, a light directly above it, and a door set off to the side that was almost hidden in the design of the panelling. I marched up to the window, trying to look official. They had pulled a beige shutter down behind the window, but there was an old-fashioned bell with a plunger on top. I had always wanted to have a go on one of these, and I tapped it twice. The shutter rolled up with a snap and a female Grenlik looked through the window. "Yes?"

I was already standing up as tall as I could and had my serious face on. "I would speak with the Grenlik Hivemaster."

"Do you have an appointment?"

"This is SFU business. Do I need one?"

The Grenlik behind the counter glared at me for what felt like an age, and I hoped she wasn't going to call my bluff. I had nothing to back up my claim, and if anyone checked, I had just dropped myself in even deeper trouble.

"Wait here," the female snapped and pulled the shutter down as energetically as she had let it fly up. I stood in front of the window and waited. Then I stood beside the window and waited some more, leaning against the panelling and glaring back at anybody curious enough to stare at me as they passed. The unobtrusive door opened and a male Grenlik stood in the opening. I walked over to him.

"I am the Assistant Duty Hivemaster?" He seemed tense, as though he was expecting to be rejected or dismissed, but I nodded and he stepped aside to let me in to what turned out to be a small, bare room with a table and four chairs. In the wall to my left was another door, which I guessed opened into the office behind the window. "What is your business?" he asked once we sat.

I had been thinking about this while they kept me waiting, realising one chance to say the right thing. "I am here on behalf of Warrior Jones. She requires something from the room your Hivemaster has been kind enough to offer her."

"This is not our concern."

I nodded. "Of course, but it would be rude of me simply to walk in and wander around without asking your permission and, to be honest, I would appreciate a guide to show me where the room is. The directions Warrior Jones gave me were... brief," and I smiled to let the Assistant Duty Nobody know I was letting him in on a little secret. His expression didn't change, so I wasn't sure it had worked, but after a moment he nodded.

"We appreciate your consideration. If you wait here for a moment, I will guide you myself." He stepped through the door into the office, there was a muted conversation, and he reappeared – this time wearing an overcoat. He opened the outer door and gestured. "Would you follow me, please?"

I did, out of the room, past the guards at the bottom of a staircase, and up three levels. From there, we went through another door and I realised I had no idea which direction I was facing.

The light level behind this door was even lower, and it took my eyes a few seconds to adjust. Wall sconces, yards apart, had tiny balls of glowing magic. The walls looked made of brick, arching overhead like a tunnel, and the air was humid. It smelt earthy, like a forest. Doors opened off both sides, each opposite one of the infrequent lights, and between every second door on the inner side, a corridor stretched off into the hive. Muted sounds of speech, and brighter sounds that might have been children playing, echoed along the corridor, but nobody came through any door I could see. The corridors vanished into the distant shadow, and I guessed they went the entire width of the building.

A few steps later, we stopped outside a door I thought might be in a corner of the building. There was an uncomfortable pause, and neither of us moved. This was the biggest part of my bluff. "The door, please?" I said, like it was obvious I would expect him to unlock it for me. Either that, or I had to get him to leave, then try breaking in. Less than ideal. I had already drawn too much attention to myself, and convincing the undermanager to let me in would be a much better idea if I could pull it off.

"But...?" the Grenlik said, looking panicked. I kept still, trying to stare him down, and make him think I had no intention of going anywhere until he had opened the door for me. Eventually, he lowered his eyes. The set of his jaw made it clear he didn't enjoy being treated this way, but he reached into a pocket and took out a short rod. The handle was wooden, but the business end was smooth, matt black, and seemed to absorb what little light there was. I didn't like it and wouldn't have taken it if he'd held it out to me. A shiver ran along my spine.

The Grenlik slid the rod into a matching hole in the door, and there was a positive click from somewhere near the handle. He turned the knob and pushed the door open. I took two steps inside, then turned, holding onto the door and blocking the way for the undermanager.

"Thank you. I can find my own way back from here."

"But —?"

"Sorry, this bit is confidential. Warrior-only classified." My powers of improvisation started to run out of ideas, and I just wanted to bustle the Grenlik away as fast as I could. "Or you can wait outside, if you like?" I added.

The Assistant Duty Hivemaster shook his head. "That won't be necessary. If that's all...?"

I gave him one of my best smiles. "You've been most helpful. I shall be sure to tell Warrior Jones."

The Grenlik bobbed a bow and scurried away. I shut the door. There was a bolt inside, and I pushed it across, then I turned and sagged against it, not sure I could walk across the room for a moment or two.

It was almost dark in the room. A little of the weak daylight struggled around the edges of a heavy drape over the window. I pulled the curtain aside turned on every lamp I could find, but it made little difference. I picked the magic-powered torch out of my pocket and started to search.

There wasn't much to look through. There was a single bed, a table beside it, and a wardrobe with a drawer at the bottom. Next to the wardrobe was a small table with a single chair. The floorboards were bare wood, and the walls were like those outside. With the better light from the torch, I could see that the brickwork was fake, like textured wallpaper.

I looked over the bed first, plumping the pillow and lifting the mattress to check that she'd hidden nothing inside or under either. Next, I pulled open the drawer in the bottom of the wardrobe, and found a change of clothes, a towel and a wash bag. The wardrobe itself was equally uninteresting and contained even less: a few lonely hangers and a pair of boots. There was a built-in shelf, just above my eye-line, but when I stood on tiptoe and swept my hand across it, all I got was a layer of grey dust over my sleeve. I brushed at it, annoyed, as I looked around the room. There had to be more to see than this?

The drawer deserved a second look, and I rummaged through, wishing I had gloves as I gave each garment a closer inspection. It wasn't that I thought Evie was dirty, I just wasn't comfortable messing with somebody else's underwear. Still, I picked up every item and shook it before putting it back on the other side of the drawer. Last, hidden in the corner, was a pair of socks twisted into a ball. I was about to drop them on the other pile when they felt wrong in my hand, so I squeezed the socks again. Something inside crinkled, so I took them over to the bed and unrolled them. Nothing fell out, but something still made a noise. I turned each sock inside out, and from one fell a slip of paper.

There was something written on it, and I turned it over and smoothed it out. There were letters, but they made no sense. Disappointed, I folded the paper and tucked it away in a pocket. So far, it looked like I had hit a dead end. I turned around and sat on the bed so hard I bounced, lips pursed in frustration and shoulders slumped. It was so annoying. I saw more dust on my sleeve and brushed it away as I glared at the wardrobe. The strokes got slower, then stopped. Something was nagging me about the cupboard.

Nineteen

It took me a while. I looked all through it again, but there was nothing out of the ordinary. Then I realised what bugged me wasn't inside, it was outside. And it wasn't the wardrobe, it was the floor next to it. It wasn't much, just that there was less dust on one side than the other.

But when I took out my torch and shone it on the floor, there were tracks that came sideways from under the wardrobe. They were no more than a slight indentation in the floorboards, two pairs of them, and each a half-inch wide. Either something was supposed to move out of the bottom, or the entire wardrobe slid sideways.

A quick check of the side panel eliminated the first option, so I stepped to the side away from the floor marks, put my hands against the wardrobe, and pushed. I didn't expect it to work. There would be a lock inside somewhere I would have to find, either a simple catch, or something more complicated, with a key.

Except the wardrobe rolled smoothly to the side and revealed a door. A small door, almost a hatch, set back an inch into the wall.

It was such an insignificant door, I probably wouldn't have paid it much attention. It looked like something to hide those holes up buildings where they ran pipes and wires and things.

But that someone needed to hide it, and put wheels under a wardrobe to do so, meant there was no way I could leave it alone.

But there was no handle, only a hole just too small to poke my pinkie in, and that meant a key. I hadn't seen one, either human- or Grenlik-style, nor anything else that would fit the hole—but I hadn't been looking for one. I worked the room over again.

And found nothing. If Evie had any secrets behind that door, she would be better at hiding them than I would ever be at finding them. Frustration mixed with the growing idea that this might be a dead end, and that I had no more clues to follow to help my friend. I sat on the bed and felt miserable.

Except a few minutes later, I realised I was staring at the wardrobe, and that it was bugging me. I had a thing about wardrobes. Not monsters jumping out of them. I had the Narnia thing of dreaming they were portals to hidden places. But there was something else, too.

When I was a little girl, I always had an irresistible urge to know what I was getting for Christmas. I would search high and low, especially in places I wasn't supposed to go. No cupboard or closet was safe, every drawer and wardrobe got investigated in case of secrets concealed within. Then, one year, it stopped. All the presents disappeared and I remember everybody going around looking smug as I got more and more frustrated, then terrified I wasn't getting anything at all. I hadn't been able to find a single thing, and every present that year, and the next, had been an absolute surprise.

And all this was coming back to me because the wardrobe in Evie's room looked very much like to the one tucked away in the spare room of my grandparents' house. The wardrobe was where I eventually found my presents. Crossing the room, I prodded at the chair to check it would take my weight, placed it next to the wardrobe, and stepped onto it to explore the top.

There was a deep decorative edge running all the way around the top, leaving a space three inches deep hidden from the ground. I swept my arm back and forth, but all I collected was more dust. I moved the chair to the other side and tried again. This time my fingers brushed something, and I stretched as far as I could to get a better grip. I managed to drag it closer, then my fingers felt a cube, about three inches across, and I stretched my fingers over it to pick it up. Something inside moved.

The chair wobbled, and I decided to jump, rather than step, down to the floor. I took the box over to the window, where the light was best, and saw it was made from strips of a pale wood. I tilted the box from side to side to make the contents slide about. Whatever was inside, there was only one of it. I turned the box over and over, but there was nothing identifiable as a lid, and I wondered if it was a puzzle box. I went back to the bed, sat down, and started trying to figure how it opened.

It wasn't easy. I made a strip on one face move a fraction of an inch, but it didn't seem to release any of the other sides. Still, it was a start. In the near-darkness, I held the cube close to my face, trying to get a better look at what I was doing, and nearly dropped it. It was almost dark outside.

I checked my watch and gasped. Thirteen hours; two longer than I had ever stayed before. My snap-back limit had been tested to its limit yet, and I would probably be fine, but if I jumped out now, it would be thirteen hours before I could come back. Thirteen hours before I could do anything else useful. I took a deep breath and decided to give it one more hour.

My magic torch was just too big to hold in my mouth, so I propped it on Evie's pillow and made do. Keeping an eye on my watch fragmented my focus, but I made slow progress. Then, in a rush, four secrets fell in quick succession and the box sprung open. Literally. The last movement was vigorous and whatever was inside flew across the room, then rolled under the wardrobe. I swore under my breath and jumped after it.

Lying on the floor, I banished any creepy crawly thoughts and swept my arm as deep under the wardrobe as I could reach. The gap wasn't enough to get my entire arm in, and my fingertips brushed something that rolled away. I swore again, knowing there was nothing I'd seen in the room I could reach underneath with.

Calmly rising to my feet, I pushed the wardrobe out of the way, retrieved the object, and slid the wardrobe back to the reveal the door—all the time feeling grateful nobody was there to see how stupid I could be.

There were ten minutes before my hour was up, but I couldn't quit now. What I picked up looked like a broken peg, the old-fashioned type for hanging washing out, that sort of look like a dolly with a head and two legs. Except someone had snapped one leg off, and the other had small dents in it about halfway up.

It fit the hole in the door, and I felt it engaged with some mechanism deeper inside. It was hard to turn without a proper handle, but I wrapped the sleeve of my coat over it and got a better grip. Once I got it moving, the lock turned easily.

And behind the door was a steep flight of narrow stairs—or a ladder with wide rungs. Neither appealed to me, but I couldn't stop now. I checked my watch and saw I was out of time, but no way was I going home until I saw what was so important at the top of those stairs.

That turned out to be a trap door, which meant I might be coming down backwards. I gave it a shove with one hand, the other planted on the top step to keep me stable. It wasn't too heavy, but one-handed was a bit of a struggle. A rope I hadn't noticed kept it from falling all the way open. It was all a bit complicated climbing out, which is why I didn't notice it until I had got myself all the way out.

It was a clockface, half as tall again as I was, made up of black edging and clear glass. I stopped and stared, edging closer, my fear of heights somehow forgotten. It was the clock I saw when I was outside, looking up from the ground—except that had white panels. I tried to puzzle it out, then let it go and filed it under 'weird Underland magic stuff'.

The view across UnderLondon was incredible. I could see the Tower in the distance, and the low bridge where Tower Bridge should have been, and Hyde Mountain only took up a sliver of the view on the right-hand side. Evie must love it up here, and I understood why she kept it a secret.

I turned away from the clock window and saw a table, a chair, and a waterfall of paperwork. This was where Evie had hidden everything important. This was what she had been working on, and what I had to go through to see what could have happened to her.

But I had to go, and I hadn't even time to get back to my locker at the Tower to dump all my gear. I looked over my shoulder at the clock and realised I had a way out. The image of that clock was already imprinted on my mind—at least until the Underland memory thing erased it—and I knew I could jump back here any time I wanted.

I stripped out of my Warrior clothes and hung them over the chair. At least that would let Evie know she was being looked for if she was in hiding or something. The PPG and the holster, and all the other small items I put on the table like paperweights. But I couldn't jump out from here. I backed down the stairs, closed the trap door, and hurried down to the other room. After locking the hatch behind me, I pushed the wardrobe back into place and I was just about to toss the key onto the top of the wardrobe when I realised it didn't have the extra security of the puzzle box. I looked around for it, but a desperate urgency welled up in my chest, as strong as a panic attack. Was something telling me to get out, and right then? I decided not to argue with it and snapped back into my bedroom.

I sighed, dropped the peg onto my bedside table, and fell back onto the bed. It was only just after breakfast, but I had been up for hours—very busy, stressful hours—and I felt drained. With my legs still dangling over the side of the mattress, I closed my eyes. Just for a minute.

The smell of warm food hung in the air when I woke, and the light coming in through my windows confused me for a moment, telling me it was both first thing in the morning and early afternoon. Looking at the clock on the bedside table didn't help. It told me 5:22. My stomach cramped, and hunger made the time a moot point. I set off in search of the food.

It was still Saturday, and the food was our evening meal, which on this occasion was a vegetable pasta bake with garlic ciabatta bread and ice cream for dessert. We ate off lap-trays, watching the television. I devoured the meal and fielded parental small talk asking if I was feeling OK and was anything going on at school I wanted to talk about.

"After all," said my mum. "I know teenagers are supposed to enjoy their sleep, but napping right through the day isn't like you."

"Honestly, Mum. I'm fine. I've been reading a fantastic book and I guess I stayed up a bit too late a bit too often."

Mum looked unconvinced but didn't press. All I could think about was the clock room and the mountain of papers. They had to be important. Evie wasn't tidy, but she also wasn't the type to keep paperwork unless it meant something to her. But whatever it was, I couldn't do anything more about it until first thing tomorrow morning, which was the earliest I could jump back in, and that was a double horror: Monday, and a school day.

Twenty

I was sitting on the bench outside the toilets. Lunch was a memory, and I was trying to read from my iPad. My mind kept drifting back to the clock room, and the piles of paper to investigate.

Something made me look up. Melanie Styke was walking towards me, complete with a couple of the older girls in her group and a boy I recognised as an Observer, but who didn't go to our school. There was something in the way Styke was holding herself that made me sit up and put my iPad away.

When Styke stopped, she was well inside the boundary of my personal space. I had left it too late to stand up, so all the girls loomed over me and I couldn't shake the sense of intimidation that mixed with the anger growing inside me.

"What is this Styke? Piss off or—"

"This is official, Stone, so I suggest you shut your mouth and listen for a change."

I looked up at the boy and he gave me a small nod. I tried to relax and settled back. Styke took a many times folded sheet of paper out of a pocket and shook it until it unfurled. Then she read from it, a huge smile on her face, and making sure everybody around her could hear every word.

"By order of Aslnaff, Administrator of the Special Facilities Unit, Claire Stone is hereby given notice that she has been suspended from the SFU pending investigation related to actions unbecoming a member of the Unit and in contradiction to both Unit written procedures and specific instructions given to her by lawful officers of the Unit. Ms Stone is required to attend a hearing of the council of the SFU in two weeks, at SFU headquarters. If Ms Stone enters Underland anywhere other than the administrative offices, she does so without the protection of the SFU or any other authority.

"Ms Stone is required to surrender any and all devices in her possession to the bearer of this notification."

Styke re-folded the paper and looked up. "So I'll have that Kevlar off you for a start, loser" she said, vicious grin wide on her face.

"Like hell you will," I said, trying to get to my feet. The two older girls took a step forward and one put a hand on my shoulder, pushing me back onto the seat.

"Don't," the boy said, and everybody froze, not sure who he was talking to. "Back up. All of you."

They did, though it was obvious they were reluctant to pass up such an excellent opportunity for a quick bully.

"I don't have it with me," I lied. "You know the regulations on taking artifacts out of Underland."

"Crap. You're wearing it. We're all wearing them."

"You can't take it from me. Try and I'll scream loud enough to get a teacher over here and the lot of you will get done for bullying." I scowled at Styke. "And they'll rip that prefect's badge off you."

Styke laughed. "Think so. Who do you think they'll believe? A prefect, or a weirdo like you?"

The boy turned to Styke. "If you try to force her to hand it over, I'll back her. And I don't care if you grass me up to Aslnaff, Shite. I'm here because it's official, but I don't have to like it. Or you." He turned back to Claire. "Look, I know she's evil spawn, and getting off on this, but it is official. If you don't hand it over, they'll booby trap it. It's useless to you."

"How?"

"Not sure. Never happened before, as far as I know. Supposed to be they act like Tasers if you jump in anywhere except headquarters. You get frozen until someone comes and releases you."

"You must have heard about Warr—"

"Not my problem." The boy interrupted, and his face went from helpful to blank in an instant. "Look, in a month or so you won't remember anything about any of this, so what does it matter?"

I looked up at Styke, holding her gaze as long as I could, desperately trying to think of anything I could do other than give in, but I came up blank. Reluctantly, I raised my hands and felt for the clasp at the back of my neck.

Styke's expression shifted toward triumphant as I lifted the amulet out from under my shirt, and the prefect held her hand out toward me, eyes shining like she was stealing my soul. I moved my hand forward, then snatched it back, now wearing a grin of my own.

"Where's my receipt?"

"What," Styke snapped, annoyed.

"If I was handing this into stores, I'd get a receipt. I want one from you."

"Oh, stop screwing around and give it to me."

"She has a point," said my inconsistent advocate, and there was a general rummaging about as someone found paper and someone else donated a pen. By the time a suitable document was scrawled out, I'd got to my feet. I'd no intention of running. If what they were saying about the amulet was true, there was no point keeping it anyway, but I was not going to let Styke screw me over like this while I was sitting down like a victim.

"Now give me the Kevlar." Styke was almost shouting as she held out the tatty piece of paper. Claire snatched it out of her hand and made a show of reading it. "Your handwriting looks like a six-year-old's," I said, and made a *pfft* noise at it. Petty, I know, but I had to take something back from her. "Would have looked better in crayon, but I suppose it's close enough. Here." I tossed the amulet to the floor at Styke's feet.

"Clever," said Styke, but she still bent over to pick it up. I was already walking away, but I walked just close enough so that with a swing of my hips I sent Styke sprawling onto the gravel. There was a chuckle mixed with Styke's outraged shriek. "I'll get you for that, Stone."

"Any time, *Runner*," I said, waving airily over my shoulder like I didn't care, and I was sure I heard the chuckle again. I took the first entrance I found back into the school, then headed for the nearest toilet. By the time I got there, my whole body was shaking and spasms of pain dug into my kidneys as my back muscles clenched. In the mirror over the sinks, my face was white apart from two spots of pink over my cheek bones. A splash of cold water didn't help, and the room spun around me. A moment later, my lunch was in the sink and I was washing out my mouth at the water fountain.

Sitting down in a cubicle, I jammed the door shut with my foot and dropped my head into my hands. That had been the most humiliating event in my life, and what was I going to do about Evie? The first sob came despite everything I tried to stop it, and after the first broke through, I had no chance of stopping the others. I cried, silently, sitting on the toilet until the bell rang for lessons. More cold water on my face from the sink did nothing to hide my red eyes, and I grimaced at myself in the mirror before I set off for my next class.

TWENTY-ONE

It was Wednesday before I could make myself jump into the clock room. I'd avoided thinking about it since Monday and refused to watch any news. I couldn't bear seeing anything that might remind me that Evie was still missing, and that there was so little I could do about it. Both nights I had nightmares about suffocating or drowning and had woken gasping for breath.

Trying to get back to sleep had been impossible. Every time I was about to drop off, it felt like my heart missed a beat, or a breath out felt like it would never become a breath in. By Wednesday night, I realised I had to do something to get rid of Evie's ghost. I almost fallen asleep in class twice, and my bed was calling to me even now, though I was terrified of it.

So after dinner I went up to my room, claiming I had homework to do. I pictured the clock room, but the jump failed miserably. For a moment, I thought my old problems had come back to haunt me, but after a few seconds of honest thought, I knew why. I was jumping into Underland without a Kevlar, defenceless, and with no support from the people I used to rely on. The idea terrified me.

But I was jumping into a space I figured was probably one of the safest in UnderLondon and, once I convinced myself of that, I tried again. This time I got in, though the jump felt rough, and I stumbled a couple of steps when I arrived.

It was impossible not to get drawn to that awesome view as soon as I arrived. The sun was on its way down and cast a long shadow from the clock tower. I could only look for a few minutes, though. Unless I wanted to work in the dark.

I groaned when I turned to look at the chaos I inherited. There was paper all over the table, and for a yard in every direction around. A second chair, on the other side of the table, was piled high too. Much of it was ordinary, photocopier sized sheets, but mixed in were sheets the size they use on the tilted draughting boards. Evie had folded some, rolled others, and I couldn't see even a hint of organisation.

Which didn't mean it wasn't. Evie probably knew where every sheet of paper was and what was on it. But I didn't, and if there was a clue in any of this to help me find her, I had no option but to go through it one sheet at a time and impose my own idea of order onto the mess.

I picked up a few sheets and stared helplessly at them for a moment, then noticed what I thought was a mound of paper wasn't. Whether deliberate or accidental, a pile of paper had fallen over and hidden something beneath. I pulled out a battered, mid-sized sports bag with a busted zip, and put in on the empty chair. Pulling the opening wider, I peered inside. Everything was a muddle, mostly of paper, and I wasn't keen on plunging my hand inside. It would be safer to lift the bag by its ends, turn it upside-down, and shake everything out onto the floor. I moved away from the paper chaos to a clear area and did just that.

It was a jumble; several tightly bundled fabric somethings, a towel, some old newspapers, a document wallet, one reasonably innocuous trainer and a tube of tennis balls. The tube was still sealed, so that went straight back into the bag, as did the trainer once I turned it upside-down and shook it.

The newspapers were from the Over and were three months old. I flicked through them, but there seemed to be nothing of obvious interest, so I put them aside. Maybe I could get them into a recycling box later.

That left the papers and the two fabric lumps. I hoped they were tee shirts, but just to be safe, I picked the first up with finger and thumb. Evie had wrapped it around something and as I lifted it into the air, it unrolled. Before I could get my other hand around to catch it, the enclosed something fell to the floor. It was a bit bigger than a smartphone, and much thicker, and there was a hint of a button on the side.

The wrapping could have been to protect it or to stop anyone touching it by accident. Not knowing which, I used the tee-shirt as a glove to turn it over. It had fallen face down. Along one edge, which I assumed was the top, were the letters "LMFDA- Mk 4A". Below that was a transparent window with a needle inside over a series of scales. Across the middle was a sliding switch, with positions labelled from "x.01" to "x100", so maybe it measured something. What that was, I had no idea. The fingers of my right hand wiggled as I toyed with the idea of pushing the button to see what would happen, but I rolled the meter up in its tee-shirt and put it aside. No point tempting fate. Yet.

I was more careful with the other bundle and unwrapped it rather than letting it unroll. The contents were just as much contraband, though much more familiar. Even so, I used the wrapping to pick up and examine what appeared to be a perfectly normal, if old, pair of Warrior goggles. I folded the tee to make a cushion, put it next to the meter, and rested the goggles on top, safe and out of the way.

Now all that I had left was the document wallet, which was stuffed full and held closed by elastic bands. I weighed it in my hands and debated if I even wanted to open it. It looked like there were pages and pages and it could be personal stuff I had no right sticking my nose in. But if I started, I would have to look at everything, and it would be dark soon. If I took it home, I could work on it there, but would have to be careful not to raise any parental questions. I was just trying to decide whether I should take the who bag or just the folder when the room lit up.

I dropped to the floor, crouching down in case anybody saw me, and looking around for where the damned light was coming from. No way could I jump out, scrunched up like this. And then I realised it must have been like this during my first visit, and it hadn't registered. But it didn't explain where the light came from. There were no lights on the walls or ceiling, but then I noticed my shadow was pointing away from the clock. Was the light outside? When I turned, that wasn't what it looked like. If anything, it looked like it was the clock itself that glowed, but that made no sense. For anyone to see it from street level, it should have been blinding in here, which it wasn't. I turned around until I was staring at the face of the clock. Was I being too logical, too Over? Underland was weird, which my face had been rubbed in too many times to count. How would they do it? They'd probably use magic to make every pane of glass collect light in the day and reflect it out at night. Was the light inside just leakage?

Keeping to the edge of the clock, so I wouldn't stand out if someone looked up, I walked closer until I could touch a panel on the clock face. My fingers tingled when they touched it, like electricity, then it just felt warmer than it should. I looked closer and saw a dazzling thin line around the edge.

It was as good an explanation as any, and I let it go at that, hoping the glass was one-way too. Everything I needed was far enough back that anyone would have to be almost at the same height to see me inside. I went back to the table and cleared it off. I almost swept it all off with my arm, which was something

I always wanted to try, but it would make even more mess. It made more sense to lift it off in stacks, and to keep it all relative to itself.

The tidying took longer than I expected, and it was harder work, and all just to move a mess rather than resolve it. Scowling, I picked the folder up from the floor and took it over to the empty table. The elastic bands felt gritty and snapped as I tried to ease them off. Opening the flap and peering inside, I saw a confusion of paper and sighed. This would take a while.

The paperwork fell into three groups; there were sheets that were maps, sheets that looked like official reports, and lots and lots of notes scrawled on various scraps of paper. I sorted them into three piles and made a note to bring some bulldog clips to hold the piles together. The reports and the notes looked dry and boring, so I put them aside in favour of the maps.

Tiredness washed over me, and I started to think it was time to turn in. Being stressed out all the time made me restless, and it seemed stupid to ignore feeling tired. Maybe I could catch up on sleep and not feel so beaten in class. I flicked through the sheets of map I had stacked together as I tried to decide if bed was the right option. Some were pristine, whilst others had marks on them. I stopped, frowned, and turned back a few pages. The frown deepened as I flicked back and forth, then my eyes opened wide, and any thoughts of an early night faded. All the separate sheets were one big map. It was a jigsaw.

I started to lay the pieces out on the floor, but they kept moving like there was a current of air too light for me to feel. I needed sticky tape, clips, pens, and I was hungry, which meant I needed to jump home for supplies.

Mistake.

As soon as I appeared in my bedroom, I almost dropped to my knees, I was so tired. Maybe it was a good thing, and I certainly didn't want to tempt fate. Everything would be there for me tomorrow, but for now I quickly changed into my night things, crawled into bed, and dreamed I was an ant trapped on a paper map.

After school the next day, I tried to run straight up to my room as soon as I got into the house. Hours of thinking about the map, rather than the lessons, gave me an idea, but Mum intercepted me in the kitchen. "Your father and I are going out tonight. Will you fix yourself something, or shall I cook, and you can reheat it?"

It took me a moment to switch my thoughts away from the map and to wrap my mind around the random thought. I took the berry tea Mum offered me and slowly turned the mug around and around.

"You'll spill that," she said, making my head jerk up. "Now, what about the food?"

"I'll do a sandwich, or something," I said, hoping that was the end of the conversation and shifting my weight ready to slide off the breakfast stool. Mum gave me a parent-look and shook her head, but I made my escape and hurried up to my room to sort out supplies of tape and clips—and my wind-up travel alarm clock.

My folks called out they were leaving, and I yelled back a barely coherent farewell as I realised now would be a good time to fix something to eat. The office supplies, together with a bottle of water and a cheese and tomato sandwich, ended up in a plastic bag, and a moment later they were in the clock room with me. Putting the food aside, I took out the sticky tape, dropped to my knees, and started putting the map together.

I started to lay the pieces out on the floor, splitting them into areas I knew and others I didn't before lining the edges up. It got more complicated as the sheets left were of places I had never been and before long I was hunting for matching street names along the edges. A few places had missing pages, which cost me time to check and recheck. It took hours to finish. And when I was done, I stood over it.

And had to admit it made no sense at all.

I mean, it made sense as a map, but it didn't make any sense why Evie had made it. There was writing on it in several places, but it was just symbols, letters or numbers and had no meaning to me.

I wasn't in the best of moods when I got up, brushing the dust off my jeans before I grabbed the bag of food and dropped into the chair at the table. As I munched, I pulled the folder closer, opened it, and took out the main bundle of papers. Everything else was loose fragments. I pulled the clip off the top and started leafing through the sheets. They still looked like some stuffy reports, but they were uneven, and the print was crooked. Whoever had copied them had been very sloppy, or in a hurry. Quality aside, everything was numbers or abbreviations, and the only thing I came close to recognising was "LMFD", and that was only because the same sequence appeared on the gadget hiding in a drawer in my room.

I sighed and picked up the reports before shuffling them into a neat stack and clipping them together again. Evie had gone out of her way to hide this collection of the strange, bizarre, and utterly boring. It must have meant something to her. Enough for her to want to keep it safe, anyway. Or was I getting everything turned around? Maybe this was just a bag of junk that Evie had been meaning to get rid of. I picked up the folder and was about to slide the reports back in when I saw the loose sheets I hadn't looked through yet.

Tilting the folder, I let them slip onto the table. Every scrap seemed to have Evie's handwriting on it. I turned everything face up and laid it out in rows before putting my elbows on the table and my chin in my hands as I scanned across the last of the haul.

Five minutes later, I was scowling again and muttering curses under my breath about Evie wasting my time and being awkward, obnoxious and obstructive. Nothing stood out and nothing made any sense. I saw lists of numbers that looked as though she might have taken them from the reports, but everything else was either in code or shorthand. Nothing seemed to match up with the symbols on the map. Suddenly furious, I picked up the scattered notes and stuffed them on top of the reports in the folder. I wasn't even going to bother taking this junk to the recycle. This was Evie's mess, and she could fix it, or the Grenlix who rented her the room could. Either way, I was done.

Then something felt different in my fingers. At first it looked like a compliments slip, but as I looked closer, it turned into a long, thin envelope. The flap was tucked in, rather than glued down, so I flipped it open, cupped my hand underneath, and gently squeezed the sides of the envelope. A single sheet of paper slid out. The only reason I gave it any attention was how different it was: uncrumpled, precisely folded, and clean.

And there were words. Whole words. And recognisable dates. And the words were street names. Some I even recognised, and there were numbers that referred back to the pages of the report. I grabbed the notes from the table and knelt next to the map. I was still cross-referencing pages when my alarm clock went off. It was set to ring after eight hours, to stop me from losing track of time. My luck was seriously pushed last time, testing my snapback to its limit, and I didn't want it to happen again. I looked at the map and the paper, feeling the answer was right at the tips of my fingers, but knowing it might still be hours away. At least I didn't have to clean up. I grabbed my things and headed home.

Twenty-Two

I might not have got a lot of sleep over the past two nights, but it was quality sleep and I felt loads better for it. Yesterday, I jumped in as soon as I got back from school again. With the list I found in Evie's notes, things started making sense. Each mark on the map corresponded to a line on the list. The dates went back a year and seemed to be days where there had been an incursion. I remembered two of the dates because I'd been involved, so I assumed the others were the same.

The incursions clustered around a few specific areas, but each report in each location was several months apart. Almost every incursion linked to at least one page of the incomprehensible report. Of the half-dozen that didn't, Evie had written some numbers against them herself. It still made as much sense to me as algebra to a hamster.

The list changed at the bottom of the page. Here were eight addresses, with no dates or other notes. Evie had crossed four out in no apparent order, and they made up a second set of symbols on the map. Claire guessed Evie had been visiting the places on that list. Maybe she had gone missing while she was visiting one of the four that weren't crossed out yet. But which one?

My first thought was to take the documents to the council; to get Aslnaff and the police to see that there was something wrong and force them to do something. Then I remembered how dismissive Aslnaff had been. Even with all this evidence, would he change his mind? He didn't seem to be the type who could admit he had made a mistake. And there were the lengths Evie had gone to hide the paperwork. She wanted this information safe. She was protecting it from somebody, or protecting herself from some consequence of owning it.

Evie had a list of a dozen places, eight of which she had drawn lines through, which meant one of the last four was where she went missing. The only way to figure out which one was to go look for myself.

I woke up this morning with the decision already made. I was going to jump into Underland and explore. A few hours poking around, snap back, and get ready for school. Easy. A few minutes later I was wearing Warrior-chic, armed, and terrified by the thought of having no Kevlar. But then, nobody else knew and so long as I acted the part, nobody need find out. I stood straight, pulled my shoulders back, and crabbed inelegantly down the ladder to the room below. Only when I had my hand on the door did I realise I couldn't lock it behind me. I was figuring out if I had time to do a standard jump back home, then come back in to somewhere I knew—which had its risks. I had already been gone fifteen minutes, and if anybody came looking for me in that time, I would need some pretty convincing lies—when I saw a key hanging from a nail hammered into the back of the door. It made sense, in a way. Evie would only ever need the key if she was in the same position as I was. I took it off the nail, let myself out, and tucked the key in my pocket as I strode towards the stairs. Once I was out through the door at the corner of the building, I turned back and looked up. For once, my memory was being honest with me, and the face of the clock was white. One way, and very clever. Feeling smug, and a little safer, I marched down the street. Time usually matched between the Over and Underland, at least after jumping in, so it was still early and the streets were quiet and unhurried. A tram puffed past me, heading towards Old Street, but most of the traffic was hand carts and pedestrians. The air smelt crisper than usual, as though it hadn't been used too much yet, and the sky was almost white. Nobody seemed interested in me, or what I was doing, which suited me perfectly.

The first address, in Hoxton Road, was a total bust. I snooped around outside, and even bullied my way past the doorman to check out the basement, but the trail was old and useless. I checked my watch. That waste of time had cost me an hour and had been so frustrating that I toyed with the idea of jumping out and going to school. That made me stop and think. When had going to school ever been more interesting—and less frustrating—than being in Underland? I pulled the list out of my pocket to check before I left, caught my bottom lip between my teeth when I saw the next address, and changed my plans.

The station could not have looked more different. People wandered through the ticket halls even though it was early, and there was a rumble of noise drifting up from the bottom of the escalators that hinted of rushing trains. I stopped at the top of the escalators, standing between them and trying to keep out of peoples' way. I needed a moment before I could bring myself to go down to the platform.

My memories were so sharp as they flooded back to me. Fear tried to tie a knot in my gut and made me breathe in short, shallow gasps. That left me dizzy and added to the growing panic. I closed my eyes and forced my breathing into a slower, deeper rhythm. Moments later, my heart stopped feeling as though it was either going to jump from my throat or straight out of my chest and finally I could step across onto the down-escalator.

At the bottom, I stood in the middle of the small hall and held Evie's old goggles over my eyes, while Underkin grumbled as they eddied around me. I ignored them and turned in a slow circle. The only traces of Morph activity I could see were vague hints from the day I accidentally found the insane place, and that made no sense. I took off the goggles and walked out onto the platform. Why had Evie been interested in the place if nothing had happened here for so long? When I pushed the goggles over my eyes again to check the platform and to look out along the tunnel, they showed the same story. It made very little sense.

"Oy." The voice was nasal and irate. I turned and found myself confronted by a Grenlik; short, even by their standards, wearing a scruffy uniform and looking up at me with more than enough attitude to make up for his stature. "What do you think you're doing?"

"SFU business," I replied, loftily, for want of anything better to say.

"Well stop it. You're disturbing the passengers."

"What?"

"People don't like you lot poking around. Makes them think there's something going on. Makes them nervous." I looked down the platform. Apart from a few curious glances, nobody was paying any attention to them at all now, and those that were looking seemed more interested in the Grenlik.

"I'll be as discrete as I can," I said.

"I'll make a complaint if I have to," said the Grenlik, but I had taken the wind from him when I wouldn't get into an argument. He turned and walked away, but then looked back over his shoulder. "I'll be watching you."

"Two minutes," I said, smiling at him.

He walked off, casting occasional glances over his shoulder. I stood still; watching, smiling whenever he turned back, and edging my way to the end of the platform. A train thundered past, squealing to a halt, and as soon as travellers disgorged from the doors, I spun on my heel and rushed onto the rickety ledge along the side of the tunnel.

It was easier, in the sense that this time there was no slime under my feet, but my eyes took ages to adjust from the bright light of the platform to the gloom of the tunnel. Things felt familiar, faded memories from when I had first come here to rescue Evie, but I was missing some detail. I even forgot about the steps that led from the ledge to the door until I stumbled down them, twisting an ankle.

The door was still ajar, but only just. An ordinary push didn't move it an inch. The train in the station had already rumbled off, and I could see the lights of the next train drawing closer. My head knew so long as I stayed close to the wall I would be all right, but my heart made me push frantically at the stiff door, wanting to be inside before the next train went past.

I stepped over the threshold as the train thundered by and felt the wind tug at the back of my coat. It was probably nowhere near as close as it felt, but I wasn't interested in any more detail. I fumbled the Underland torch out of my pocket and played the disc of light up and down the walls until I found a light switch, then I pulled the goggles over my eyes and followed the ancient, almost invisible trail.

There seemed to be a lot more corridors than the last time I was down here, but the air still tasted coppery and reminded me of blood. I doubted I would have been able to find the way without the trail, but the brick wall that blocked my path really didn't look right. The slime trail turned sharp left and disappeared into the wall.

I stepped back and took the goggles off. Pulling at my bottom lip, I struggled with my memory. I was sure this was where the rough, oval tunnel had branched off from the more business-like ones. And that was why the wall looked wrong. All the other walls were big bricks—'breeze blocks', my dad called them—and they looked like they were painted over and over with thick paint. But this wall was ordinary red bricks, and they weren't painted. In fact, they looked rough, and hurried, and there were splops of mortar spattered over the floor. Although I was no builder, and knew nothing about DIY, I got the feeling someone had built the wall from the other side.

"Oy!"

I groaned. It was louder, and even more irate, but unmistakably the voice of the Grenlik official from the platform.

"What do you think you're playing at? We've got trains stopped, we have, while you're mucking about down here. This is a safety issue. You can't just come running around down here, private areas and down tunnels, without proper authorisation and an escort." He had scuttled up to me, wagging a finger in front of me to make his points. He stopped right in front of me, no more than two feet away. Only then did his rant cut off, and his eyes slid to the left, followed by the rest of his head, when he saw the wall.

"What the bloody hell is that?" He stepped over to the wall, ran his hands over it, then turned them over to look at the red dust on them from the bricks. A hand curled into a pointing finger and he turned back to me, jabbing accusingly. "What have you been up to down here? There's no authorisation for this. I don't care if you're SFU or SFA, you can't go building walls down here. I'll have your number off you, and I want you back up in my office so I can report this t—"

A moment later I was in my bedroom, then groaned when I remembered all the contraband from Underland I still carried. And I'd snapped back. I couldn't jump back in without meeting myself. I stripped it all off and jammed as much of the gear as I could into my wardrobe before running off to shower before school.

Twenty-Three

My mother took one look at me and put out an arm to stop me as I tried to breeze past when I got home from school. She laid her hand on my forehead and gave me a concerned look.

"What *have* you been doing to yourself?" she muttered. "The bags under your eyes are darker than mine."

I tried to smile, but it felt wrong on my face. "I'm OK. Just tired."

"Reading that book too long last night?"

It was a more convenient excuse than trying to make one up, so I nodded.

"Maybe you should think about having a hot soak after dinner and going straight to bed? I know this goes against every instinct in your rebellious teen soul, but it might perk you up."

"I'll think about it," I said, and nodded. Mum looked into my eyes once more, and I had to look away. It wasn't often Mum focused on the moment, but right then I could see so much in her eyes I wasn't sure how to deal with it. She gave me a push on the shoulder to send me on my way and I went up to my room. I dropped my school bag and kicked it under my desk, then I collapsed onto the bed so hard I bounced. Perhaps Mum was right. How much use would I be to Evie if I was stumbling around half asleep?

After a moment for a groan, I rolled to the edge of the bed and sat up. There was a trail to follow, and not much time. I would have to jump back in after I'd eaten. I changed into sweatpants and a tee before going down to sit in front of the TV and trying to keep myself awake watching that.

Mum woke me an hour later for dinner: pasta with grilled vegetables in a tomato sauce, delicious and filling. I zombied through the food then went up to my room, ready to visit the next address on Evie's list. Sitting on the side of my bed, I leant forward to pull on a pair of socks. A wave of dizziness swept over me. My stomach lurched and I almost tossed my dinner before I could sit up. Which I did too quick and turned the dizzy turn into a full-blown head-rush. I froze and waited until either everything settled down or I had to dive for the waste bin. My skin was clammy, and though the nausea teased at the bottom of my throat, it didn't seem inclined to go further. I rolled onto my side and pushed myself up onto the pillow. It might be best to stay down for a while until my body settled.

When I woke, it was dark. Stifling a groan, I grabbed for my alarm clock: 04:55. There was a light coverlet over me, so one of my parents must have checked on me at some point. I pushed it aside and sat up. I felt better; hungry and wide awake. Could I jump into Underland now? It would still be just as dark there. A better plan came to me and I snuck down to the kitchen. Half an hour later, I'd eaten a silent breakfast and had made myself up some sandwiches. I carried them back to my room, crept about getting dressed and collecting all my gear, then as dawn tinted the sky grey, I jumped.

The clock room was shockingly bright, but Evie's room below was almost pitch dark. I could make out just enough to see where the door was, and there was nothing I wanted from the room today, so I walked out and made my way to the entrance hall. Two Grenlix guarded the door inside. The younger of the two looked at me with curiosity, but the older seemed outraged. "The doors are closed. They open at first light."

"I need to leave now," I said. I didn't, but the longer I stood there, the more likely I would attract attention, and that I didn't want.

"The doors are closed. Humans should not be here. No good Grenlik would–"

"It's fine," I said, raising my hands peacefully. The ruckus would bring more attention than me waiting quietly in a shadow. "My apologies, Grenlix Doormaster. I shall know better in the future. The Grenlik in charge calmed down, but I saw the younger one trying to hide some amusement. Maybe I'd given the doorman a promotion, or there was no such title.

A few minutes later, I was out on the street and walking away from the hive. I dug the square of the map out from my pocket. I hadn't had time to plan a route to the next location on Evie's list, but it looked like a good thirty-minute walk.

The place looked like a building site. An eight-foot-high wall of cheap board had been put up around the perimeter, hiding the first floor of a three-storey building. There was no guard and the double wooden gates had a heavy chain holding them shut. I thought about waiting until someone came to unlock them, then remembered that kids always seemed to find a way into every building site. I figured I might as well take a walk around the perimeter while I waited for someone with a key.

The next building along had a low, decorative wall with railings along the front, almost as good as a ladder. I climbed onto them and looked into the building site. All the windows at ground level were boarded over and I couldn't see any doors. The windows above were so dark they seemed to suck light out of the air. The eight-foot drop on the other side of the fence looked huge, and the ground on the other side appeared hard and unforgiving.

I climbed over anyway.

There was one scary moment when I felt I would fall back the wrong way, but I windmilled my arms until I was balanced again, then leaned forward and pushed myself clear of the wall.

It *was* a hard landing. I hit the ground and rolled to my left, then thumped against the side of the building. My feet stung like I'd walked on nettles, and I sprawled there for a moment, catching my breath and gently moving limbs to check nothing was broken. When everything seemed to be working, I clambered to my feet and brushed the dirt off my coat before checking nothing had fallen out of my pockets.

Inside the fence, the yard was spooky-quiet, and every step I took sounded like a rhino. When I got to the corner of the building, I poked my head around for a quick look, then ducked back around the corner. There was a small courtyard between the building and the outer fence, and what might have been pillars on either side of a door. I peeked again, this time checking to see if there was a guard inside the fence, but the place still looked deserted. Keeping tight to the wall, I scurried towards the doors.

They had crushed what had once been steps and made them into a slope with hard packed earth. At the top, temporary gates of metal mesh hung from crude hinges hammered brutally into the walls. The pool of unnatural stillness was stifling, and the air felt thick in my throat. I walked up to the gates and found they were chained shut and padlocked.

I checked my watch. 07:30. If anybody was coming to work here, they would start arriving soon. I gave the chain an angry tug, and it rattled noisily. I froze. Idiot. Still, it had moved. My heart hammered as much from hope as fear. I checked the chain again, looking to see what had caused the movement, and felt a grin. Whoever had put the chain on had been careless. A loop almost a foot long was still hanging behind the gate. I pulled the slack through, as quietly as I could, until it was all on my side of the gates, then I eased the left gate open. I realised I was biting at my lower lip and forced myself to stop. It was a concentration tic, but I thought it made me look stupid, and it made my lip puff up like I'd had it plumped. Ew.

The gate came towards me with a gentle groan, matched by my own when I saw how small the gap was. I had made myself a hole less than a foot wide, which wasn't enough for me to squeeze through. I yanked angrily at the door and it wobbled, pivoting around the chain. Another, more controlled yank gave me an idea. Maybe if I only moved the bottom, it would swing out further? I dropped to one knee, tugged the gate accordingly, and it worked—except I was still too far up. My coat was going to end up a mess. I lay on the floor, pushed the gate again, and squirmed through, feeling smug.

Inside, the boards over the windows made the ground floor look as dark as night. Maybe I could have waited for my eyes to adjust, but workers were sure to be turning up soon, so I was running out of time. I pulled the torch out of my pocket and switched it on. The light from the beam seemed weaker than usual, and more yellow, but I passed it off as being an optical effect. After all, Evie told me the torch never ran out. But dim torch or not, there was no hiding the chasm in the middle of the floor.

Twenty-Four

It was a hole with a purpose. A ramp at least ten feet wide started right inside the door, and I followed it down with the beam of my torch. The ramp turned into a tunnel, then just as the beam of the torch gave out, the tunnel curved to the left. Heavy wooden trusses supported the roof, and there were wheel tracks in the dust.

Light, dim but brighter than what I was standing in, shone down a flight of stairs on the far side of the room and seemed to beckon me away from the ramp. I slid the goggles over my eyes to check if there was any nearby Morph activity and saw a blur of old trails. Some led down the ramp. Others, fresher but still weeks old, were on the stairs. They all merged into a third broad trail heading out the doors.

I didn't spend a lot of time considering options. I wasn't going down that hole unless I had to, which meant I had to explore upstairs first. The short stretch where the tunnel burrowed under the foot of the stairs made me nervous and I hopped quickly across as I ran up the first flight.

At the first landing, corridors stretched off to left and right, a dozen doors opening off each side. Some were open and they, plus the big windows at either end of the corridors, were where the light was coming from. I pulled a face. If I had to check each room, I'd be here until tomorrow.

I decided to follow the Morph trails first, and they mostly turned left. There was one ancient trace that carried on up to the next floor, but it wasn't bright enough to tempt me to follow it. I walked along the corridor and around a corner at the far end. All the doors were closed here, and it grew dim again. I swept the beam of the torch around, but it seemed even fainter and yellower than before. Just as I saw the Morph trail disappear under a door, the torch faded to nothing. That wasn't supposed to happen.

I switched it on and off a few times, slapping it against my palm for good measure, but the bulb remained stubbornly dark. If Evie hadn't already told me it worked on magic, I would have said the batteries were flat. I put the useless thing in my pocket. At least my goggles still showed me the faint, glistening trail, and even a dab of brightness on the door handle.

Cracking the door open an inch, I waited, counting heartbeats hammering in my ears and trying to listen past them for any sounds inside. I eased the door open, peering through the widening gap, ready to slam it and run if there was anything inside. Gritty light fought its way through dirty windows into a big room that looked like it was being used for storage. I pushed my goggles up and took a few cautious steps inside. Wooden crates and cardboard boxes were scattered haphazardly about, some open, and some empty or spilled. Dust hung heavy in the air, sparkling in the light and tickling my nose.

There was something about the disorder that looked unintentional. I pulled the goggles down over my eyes again and gasped. Silver confusion covered the room. It shone from just about everywhere on the floor, from most of the boxes and crates, and there were even spatters over the walls. Huge violence had happened here.

I turned a slow circle, trying to make sense of the mess, and the spatter patterns resolved themselves into two centres, each marking the violent end of a Morph. Silver covered so much of the floor that it was impossible to make out anything like trails. I pulled the goggles down and let them dangle around my neck while I turned another circle.

As my line of sight changed, the mess of boxes did that optical illusion thing where rotating nonsense turns into a face. Here, the mess resolved into a line, and at the end of the line were two dents in the wall.

The plaster had fallen away and cracked lathes stuck out like broken bones. Something hard and heavy had been thrown against the wall, and I remembered the tongue-fist attacks Morph used. As I moved closer, I saw two more of the dents, this time in the side of a wooden crate, and marks in the floor dust where the crate had been shoved aside.

"Oh, you idiot," I muttered, realising I was treading over tracks that might be useful. I stopped and squatted down for a better look at what was ahead of me. There were a couple of shapes that could have been shoe prints, but they were almost brushed out by some twisting marks. I eased forward until I could see behind it but froze and looked sharply over my shoulder. Had that been a sound?

I kept as still as I could, holding my breath and waiting to hear the noise again. Everything was quiet, apart from the faintest murmur of city life outside. I let the breath out through puffed cheeks and was about to turn back when I saw I had made the same twisting, serpentine marks in the dust. It was my coat dragging on the floor.

I let my eyes follow the imaginary line I'd seen to the next box. There was a huge dust-free square in front of it, as though it had been pushed aside. As I got closer, I changed my mind. The box wasn't pushed. Someone had knocked it over.

I stepped around the side of the box and drew in a sharp breath, my hands coming up to cover my mouth. On the other side of the box was a large smudge in the dust, then a long scraping slide. And on the wall, a foot above the floor, was a dark smear. I ran over and looked at the smudge, cursing my torch as I tried to see what colour it was. I reached towards it, flinched back, then made myself touch it. It was bone dry and even though it looked black, it had to be blood.

Standing up and turning back to face the door, I closed my eyes and a vision of what could have happened played out in my mind. The warrior running into the room, already being chased. Taking cover behind the two stacked boxes. Waiting until the Morphs followed her into the room. There had to be at least three, perhaps four. Taking a shot, bursting one. A barrage of fists, two missing, hitting the wall, one hitting the top box the warrior was hiding behind. A second shot, and another Morph disposed of, but then a strike, probably to her body, absorbed by her Kevlar but throwing her backwards into the other box and toppling it over. It would have hurt, but a Warrior wouldn't have given up. She maybe took out one more Morph, but there was no third explosion of silver. Then a last strike, the fist smashing into her, sliding her along the floor and crashing her head into the wall. Why hadn't her Kevlar protected her?

I opened my eyes and took a deep breath. My eyes pricked with moisture. The Morphs had taken Evie. Again. I shied away from the other option, telling myself there wasn't enough blood. My eyes cast around, looking for Evie's PPG. There had to be a reason she hadn't taken out a third Morph, and it could be because she had lost her grip on the gun. I saw no weapon, but a faint sparkle caught at my eye, far outside the line where everything had happened. I almost ignored it, but that something could shine on this otherwise dusty floor pricked at my curiosity.

It wasn't until I picked it up I realised what it was. Dangling from my fingers by a broken cord, its crystal black and dead, was a Kevlar amulet. Trembling, I turned it over and saw the one number I didn't want it to be.

6412.

Evie's.

Twenty-Five

I tucked the Kevlar away in an inside pocket. Now I knew why the tracks were so wide; several Morphs had followed each other. Did that mean the important track was the one going out of the building, or the one going down into the pit? Which way had they taken Evie? I took a last look around the room, just to make sure I hadn't missed anything, then retraced my steps to the bottom of the stairs. It was difficult to be sure, but it still looked as though the strongest, most recent trails went out through the gates. I made a decision and headed out of the building.

A crate against the side fence made for a convenient exit. The street was busier now, and several people stopped to watch me. I ignored them and pulled my goggles over my eyes as I made my way back to the gate.

The trail went back down St Martin's Street. I kept my head down, focusing on the trail and expecting everybody else to exercise good sense and get out of my way. There were a few muttered curses, but nobody bumped into me as I walked along.

I had no idea where I was or where I was going, but the longer the chase went on, the more uneasy I got. I had never followed a trail for this long before, especially one so weak. Doubts crept in. What if I had taken a wrong turn? There were two places where I hesitated, the right path not being as obvious as I would have liked. Could I have missed it then? Should I go back?

The trail opened out onto a major road, surprising me with how busy it was. Nose to tail carriages trundled by in four lanes, horns braying at each other. I lurched to a stop in the middle of the pavement, people of all races dodging to keep from touching me, the effect rippling outwards along the sidewalk. A quick glance at my watch confirmed I was in the middle of rush hour.

The trail went diagonally across the road, which I recognised as Piccadilly—or as close as this world came to it. I darted between two trams and ran across to the other pavement. The trail went on in front of me, passing across the front of an imposing building, then turned down a side road. I hurried after it, figuring I might as well see this trail to the end before I worried about whether I had missed a turn.

The building looked like a palace. Tall iron railings, with imposing gates, protected a wide crescent drive from the street. There were Hrund at each gate and at the door, dressed in black uniforms and looking impassive and imposing. I picked up my pace as I passed. Something about the guards' scrutiny made me uncomfortable, and I could feel eyes boring into my back as I turned down the side road.

Albany, which seemed to be all the name the alley had, slid along the side of the courtyard and palace. I could see another street at the far end, but the trail seemed to turn to the left before it got there. I took off the goggles and tried to look as though I was just strolling past.

Where the trail turned left, a ramp dropped under the wall and ended in two solid metal gates. It looked like a delivery entrance, and the two Hrund guarding it took an immediate interest in me as I passed. I tried to keep it casual, nodding and offering a neutral smile to the Hrund as I walked past the top of the ramp and on out to Vigo Street.

My knees were trembling. I needed somewhere to sit and settle myself. Something was screaming to me that Evie was inside, and something else was telling me that this time I couldn't bully or bullshit my way in. From the looks the Hrund gave me, I wouldn't even get close to them, let alone past them and into the building. I stopped and leaned against a wall, scratching my scalp with my fingernails in the vain hopes of waking up my mind. There was no escaping it; I was going to need help.

Broad Street Airship Terminus was still busy with the morning rush. The roof doors were permanently open for ships to land and depart, and I could see more ships circling the station overhead as they waited for the opportunity to disgorge their passengers. I was sitting outside a small snack food bar in a quiet corner of the concourse, facing out so I could watch the bustle. And look for Jack.

He had been the help I thought of as soon as I realised I was out of my depth, and I called him as soon as I'd been able to stop my hands shaking long enough to hold the phone-thing. He hadn't seemed pleased to hear from me and had rushed through the conversation as though he was trying to get rid of me. The location had been all cryptic hints, and even now I hoped I got it right. He was ten minutes late.

Then I saw him, striding across the concourse, and had to resist the urge to stand up and wave. He walked nervously, looking around too much. I was sure he had seen me, but it looked like he was going to walk straight past until he made a sudden turn and walked up to the café. "Hi," I said, but the rest of what I'd been going to say died in my throat, as did the idea we might hug, or even kiss. He looked *furious*.

"What the hell are you playing at?"

"Pardon?"

"Using a communicator. They can monitor those things, track you with them."

"I didn't know," I said, my eyes dropping from his face and my cheeks burning. "How else was I supposed to get in touch with you? It's not like we ever swapped mobile numbers or anything." I felt myself getting as angry as Jack looked and forced myself to calm down. "All right, I'm sorry and I shouldn't have done it that way, but I needed to talk to you."

"What about? You know you shouldn't be here, don't you? Everybody got the memo that you were suspended. Nobody in the SFU is going to help you. They won't want to get into trouble."

"Does that include you?"

The silence stretched out way too long, but Jack said, "What did you want to see me about?"

I told him most of what I had found out over the last week. Most. I didn't tell him about the gadget or the copied reports. If anybody had asked me, I wouldn't have been absolutely sure why. Jack didn't interrupt until I mentioned the exhausted Kevlar.

"It must be broken," he said. "It would have recharged."

"That's what I thought," I said. "It must have been some fight to hit it hard enough to break it."

And the story went on. When I got to the end, Jack looked pale. "At least you had the good sense not to try to get in there."

"Why?" I asked, heart sinking as I realised Jack's concerned face was not for Evie but for me, and for this palace.

"That's the Stellar Cellar. It's one of the most exclusive nightclubs in UnderLondon."

"So?"

Jack rolled his eyes. "Angels run all nightclubs, at least all the top ones, and they are all bent. They run all kinds of nastiness out of them, and Natrak Sum runs the Stellar. He's bad, even for an Angel."

I felt I ought to remember the name, but it butterflied around the edges of my memory and wouldn't make a connection. "What do you think?"

"About what?"

"Everything," I said, frowning. "What I just told you. You *were* listening?"

"I was, but it doesn't change anything."

"What? Why not?"

"No evidence."

I opened my mouth to argue but had to admit he was right. Everything I'd discovered, I'd been the only person there and even then, all I had was a gut feeling. It was all nothing more than my word. Almost. I reached into an inside pocket. "What about this?" I slapped the amulet down on the table.

With a curse, Jack leaned forward and covered it with his hand, then his brow furrowed and he picked the amulet up. "I thought you said it was dead. Drained."

"It is."

"Was, maybe, but it's fine now," he replied, turning it around so I could see the red gem on the front. It glowed a heathy red and showed full charge. Reaching into another pocked, I pulled out the torch and, looking down into the bulb, switched it on. I cried out and squeezed my eyes shut as I fumbled to switch it off again, and when I opened my eyes, a wide purple streak overlaid everything. Jack looked at me like I was an idiot. "It went flat," I explained. "In the house. It died like the battery had gone flat."

"But it's recharged, automatically, from the standing magical field—" Jack started.

"I know that, but it still stopped working," I snapped.

"How long were you using it?"

"Only ten minutes."

"Could be faulty."

I ignored him, thinking hard about something else.

"Jack, what would a LMDFA measure?"

"LM eff dee A," he corrected. "Local Magical Field Density Analyser..." His voice died away as he spoke and more ridges appeared on his brow. I told him the last details. Holding back wouldn't help Evie if it meant I couldn't get any help. "I suppose it's possible," he said when I finished. "Although it would be really, really unlikely to find a field density that low. But why would Jones be going around looking at places with a poor local field? Just to see if she could drain magical devices?"

"Help me get her out and we can ask her," I said. Jack scowled at me, but I smiled sweetly at him and waited. He gave in.

"It's near impossible," he said. "You know that, don't you? Getting into Stellar Cellar without an invite or a membership."

"There must be a way. Isn't there anybody who will help us?"

"Not officially. You need something like a tame Grenlik. They're all crooks. That's their speciality; stealth and subterfuge. That might get you something useful."

"Any other ideas?"

Jack shrugged. "Not really. I can check a few things out. See if maybe I can get some building plans, or some inside stuff on the Cellar."

"How long?"

"No idea. How long have you been here?"

I checked my watch, and it was showing a few minutes before ten. "About five hours."

"You should snap back. Wait around until about five, local time, then jump back in and meet me here. Just watch out for the commuters." He got up and threw some coins down on the table. Annoyed he had decided we finished the conversation all on his own, I got up too. Jack hesitated, fidgeted from foot to foot for a moment, then he gave me a clumsy wave and walked off. I waited until he was out of sight, wondering what it was

Jack had been trying to get the nerve to do, then walked off in the opposite direction. I still had some work to do.

Turner's Road was becoming familiar ground to me now, and I strolled down Cotton St to the shop run by Krennet Tolks. For a change, the door was open and there was a great bustling in and out. I recognised at least two of Tolks' apprentices, but the rest were strangers to me. There was a van parked outside, hissing to itself and venting a thin wisp of steam. Large objects were being carried out of the shop and into the van, all carefully wrapped in sacking.

I held back, watching but trying not to intrude. Whatever was going on was no business of mine, and there didn't seem to be any point in making trouble with Tolks by barging in on the situation. Instead, I waited until an apprentice looked up and caught my eye. I didn't see any reaction, but a couple of moments later Tolks himself walked out of the shop, casually looking around and supervising the loading. Nobody could have spotted his glance towards me if they weren't looking for it, or the three fingers he splayed across the side of his leg. I levered myself away from the wall and walked off. I had thirty minutes to idle away until Tolks was free to talk to me, or so I guessed.

When I got back, the street was empty and, to my surprise, the door to Tolks' shop was unlocked. I let myself in, closed the door behind me, and waited in the outer shop. Instead of the usual clutter, the space was almost empty and sounds seemed to chase around it like bats. When nobody came out to the front of the shop to greet me, I tried a "Hello" that sounded timid even to me.

Still there was no response, so I walked to the back of the shop and tapped at the door that led to the workshop. It moved, so I pushed it farther open and peered inside. The room was empty, apart from Tolks. He was busy pouring steaming water from a delicate silver kettle into two small cups. A strong aroma of something very like coffee filled the room. He put the kettle down on a cork coaster and gestured that I should pull one of the other stools over to his bench. I saw a soft cloth, on which were laid out a half dozen miniature tools, and a magnifier on a stand. Under the lens was a cube of grey metal, with a surface that seemed made up of cogs and moving panels. The last time I visited the workshop, he had hidden something from me, and I had a hunch this was it. I wondered why he didn't cover it this time. Once I had settled, he pushed one of the tiny cups towards me.

"You have news of Warrior Jones?" he asked, lifting his own cup and inhaling deeply before taking a delicate sip. I raised my own cup. Coffee wasn't something I often drank, but the aroma was wonderful; rich and enticing, bitter and sweet at the same time. I tried a sip, then another. The second made me shudder with the intensity of the flavour, but it wasn't unpleasant. I was less sure about the rush of heat washing out from under my breastbone, or the noticeable increase of my heartbeat. I put the cup down and took a slow breath through my nose, the air still redolent with coffee, before I spoke.

"Yes. She was taken captive by two or more Morphs while she was investigating a building site on Orange St. She was looking into dead spots in the magical field, and that was one of them."

"Do you know where they took her?"

"Maybe."

"You do or you don't. Perhaps you should start from the beginning?"

I said nothing for a moment. I was trying to keep my face neutral but think at the same time. Could I trust this Grenlik? Everything I had been told suggested Grenlix were fickle, but Evie seemed to have faith in this one. And I needed help.

"I went to Evie's room at Hive Straknat. She wasn't there, but I found some stuff she had left behind; goggles, this PPG, and a key."

"May I see that?" Tolks asked, pointing at the PPG. I handed it over. Tolks checked the safety, then examined the weapon. "This is old," he said. "Mk 18, if I am not mistaken. Six shots in the crystal, two shot fast recharge. Have you tried it?"

I shook my head. It hadn't occurred to me to shoot the thing to make sure it worked. Tolks climbed down from his stool, walked across to one of the other benches, and fitted the PPG into a clamp before attaching two devices at the stock and another over the barrel.

A moment later, the PPG started firing. I lost count of the number of times oddly constricted clouds of purple spat from the business end and, after little more than a minute, Tolks returned to the weapon and unhooked it from the gadgetry.

"The crystal is in good condition, though the emitter is slightly out of focus. The device will serve you for now."

He held it out to me, but when I reached out to take it, there was a snap like a static charge between us, like the first time we met. Tolks flinched, and I jerked my hand away, almost dropping the PPG. Had I touched him? I started a babble of apologies, but Tolks didn't look angry or hurt. He looked thoughtful. I let my apologies slow to a trickle and stop. Something felt odd about the contact. It hadn't been painful—not like when I grabbed the policeman. Tolks climbed back onto his stool, then gave me a very direct look.

"Has anything you have used in Underland done something you didn't expect it to, or that caused others to comment?"

I felt my eyebrows rise. What an odd question. What had I used apart from PPG, phone, torch, security pads, and goggles? "Nothing I can think of. Except when someone loaned me some Observer goggles to look through. He said my eyes hadn't adjusted to them properly."

"Why?"

"Oh, I saw little red streaks coming down from the sky."

Tolks was very still for a moment, then shrugged his shoulders and made a nothing sort of noise. I couldn't shake the feeling that something had happened and Tolks wasn't sharing.

"Tell me more about Jones," he said.

I told him the rest of the story. "... and then I followed the trail to a club called the Stellar Cellar."

Tolks' eyebrows clicked outwards. "Are you sure?"

"As sure as I can be following a trail more than two weeks old."

He grunted and turned his eyes down to his coffee, taking another sip. I did the same, liking it even more. When Tolks spoke, his voice was so quiet that I had to concentrate to make out the words. "I knew she was doing the survey and assumed she had no official remit. Why else would she ask me for an analyser? But how could she come to be in trouble through it? Who could have any interest in weak areas in the field except the ministry?"

"No idea," I said, not sure about half of what he said. "I mean, why would anybody want to dig a hole in the ground inside a building?"

"A what?" He sat upright and paid much more attention. I glossed over that detail, not thinking it relevant, but now I described the ramp and the curve. The Grenlik stroked the scraggy beard sprouting from his chin. "There are many reasons someone might dig such a tunnel, and none I can think of are honest. We may now know why they took Warrior Jones."

"But by Morphs?"

Tolks' mouth twisted. "You neatly drive a wedge into the weak point of my theory. It is most unfortunate. A Sum is a worthy enemy at the best of times, and Natrak is one of the more ruthless of that caste. Have you told your masters?"

"I don't think they would listen to me. I've been told to stay out of it and stay out of Underland."

Tolks chuckled, a curiously gravelly sound. "You share Jones' disrespect for authority, bureaucracy, and fools. I like that."

"How much?" I said, giving him a direct look.

"Beg pardon?"

I had surprised myself as much as him, but I knew where I was going. "How much do you like her? And me? Enough to help me get into the nightclub?"

Tolks spluttered for a moment, tried to sip the last of his coffee, and ended up in a coughing fit. "You have no idea what you are asking."

"Nope, no idea at all," I agreed, "but there is no cavalry coming over the hill. I am sure that Evie is in there, and I know I can't get myself in or her out without some real help. She had nothing but good things to say about you, and I think there is something about her you like—way more than you're telling me. What I'm asking is how far does that go? I've been told your folk are the best there is at stealth and getting in and out of difficult locations. What can I do to get you to help me?"

I flinched back as a strange look flickered across Tolks' face before it settled into a sly good humour. "I'm sure we can think of something."

Twenty-Six

Jack was waiting for me when I jumped back into Broad Street later that afternoon. I had snapped back when I finished with Tolks and, as it was still before six in the morning, I crashed and caught a couple of hours of sleep before going to school. Still, the five pm meet-up had been a challenge. Getting home in time had been a tremendous rush, as had getting changed and then jumping into Underland. I felt dishevelled and unprepared.

"What have you found out?" I asked as soon as we found seats.

"Nothing much," Jack admitted, looking unhappy. "There's not a lot about the place on file. And nobody seems to know anything about it, either. Just rumours."

I scowled. "So what can we do? We have to find a way in, or some plans for the building."

"No chance. The Cellar is a high-class affair. Only top people go there; rich, famous, or influential. Makes it easy to keep secrets."

I hesitated, not sure how my next question was going to be received. "How far will you go? With me? Tonight. I mean, breaking in, or whatever." I felt my face go bright red as I realised I hadn't chosen my words well. Jack was laughing at me again, but he got it under control quickly. Perhaps he saw I wasn't amused.

"I don't know," he said, still struggling to control a huge grin. I gave him marks for his honesty, if not for his commitment. "This could get us both in a lot of trouble. The sort you can't get yourself out of. And I'm not convinced Jones is in there. Even if she is, we have no idea where. That place is vast, and we won't be able to search all of it."

"We may not have to. We can follow the Morph trails."

"Unless they were just dropping her off."

He had a point. There were so many unknowns, and I was asking a lot of him. I, on the other hand, hadn't anything to lose.

"Do we know when this place opens?"

"Don't think it ever shuts."

It was time to let Jack in on my latest secret.

"I have some stuff that can help us."

"Like what?"

"I've a friend. A Grenlik. He gave me some gadgets. I have three things he called 'distractors', and an amulet that can make you invisible."

"You're kidding."

"Honest. He said two of the distractors were subtle, and the other wasn't."

"And the invisibility? What did he tell you about that?" There was a note of disbelief in Jack's voice, and I had to push back a flash of resentment. It was almost as though he didn't trust me, or didn't believe me.

"So long as whoever is wearing it stays out of bright light and doesn't make too much noise, it will hide them. Although he actually said "conceal". Anybody touching the one wearing the amulet gets hidden, too."

Jack's face was sceptical, matching his voice. "I'd like to see that before I trust it."

"Can't. Once it's activated, it's activated, and it only lasts about two hours. Less if it has to hide more than one person."

Jack nodded as though he'd been expecting the catch. "No surprise. Never seems to be quite what you want when you deal with a Grenlik. Whatever you paid for it, I hope it wasn't too much." He looked very directly at me, and I met his eyes. What my agreement had been with Tolks was nothing to do with him.

"I do have an idea," I said. "It's a bit of a gamble, though."

"So long as it's not trying to creep past the guards on the front door, I'll listen," said Jack.

Two hours later I was standing in a shadowed doorway on Vigo St, looking down towards the junction with Albury. Jack was tucked similarly away somewhere on Piccadilly.

I tried to make myself invisible, unremarkable, like I was projecting a shell of anonymity around me. Can't remember where I read it, but it was something like behaving how you want others to see you. I didn't know if it was nonsense, but it seemed to do something. I didn't see Underkin staring at me.

It wasn't time to use the amulet yet. Tolks warned me they were rare, and that he only had the one. Worse still, they didn't recharge on their own. All of which was a shame because I felt horribly exposed where I was. At least I had a Kevlar again. During school, I repaired the broken link on Evie's amulet and now it hung around my neck, fully charged. There had been a moment, just as I jumped in, when I wondered if Evie's amulet was booby-trapped too, but nothing tried to taze me, so I guessed not.

It was getting dark. I was feeling cold and stiff and wondering if the whole idea was the worst thing I had ever thought of when I heard, rather than saw, a delivery truck lumbering past me. Exactly what I'd been waiting for. It clinked and rattled with the clatter of a hundred glass bottles as it slowed and made the turn into Albury. As quickly as I could with fingers slightly cold-numb, I used my communicator to call Jack, and then hung up straight away. Without making myself too obvious, I hurried to the corner of Albury to be sure the driver wasn't simply taking a shortcut. He wasn't, and I saw him slowing down to take the tight turn down the delivery ramp. I made another hang-up call. By now, Jack should be waiting at the other end of Albury.

I took a distractor from my pocket. It was the one Tolks described as not being subtle. It was a tiny thing, no bigger than the oversized marbles boys used to call "3-ers" when I was a kid. I lined my thumbs and forefingers up with the four spots on the outside of the device, took a breath, and squeezed. I felt a click. Now I had sixty seconds before it went off. I dropped the marble into the gutter, just out of sight from the night club, then walked towards the ramp.

A countdown ticked in my head. The stealth amulet was already around my neck, outside my clothes, as instructed. The device was made of two discs, dark as night but with a slight dusting of silver specks across the surface of the front one. I took the two discs, one in each hand, and rotated them against each other, ant-clockwise, until I felt a click. Forty-five seconds to go.

A slight mist fogged my sight, like looking through a veil. Not enough to stop me from seeing anything, but still there. I walked across the ramp, looking down to see the doors being opened, then stood to the side and waited for Jack. Thirty seconds left. I could see him walking towards me, on the correct side of the street. He stopped where he was supposed to, and I had to stifle a giggle at him not being able to see me. I fought down an urge to touch him somewhere he wasn't expecting, like maybe his ear, then made sure nobody was looking before I reached out to take his hand. I felt him flinch, then his hand wrapped around mine and squeezed gently. Fifteen seconds.

At five seconds, I squeezed his hand every second. I'd miscounted, and the distractor went off with two seconds left. Bedlam erupted from the direction of Vigo St. There was a flash of light and the roar of a tremendous explosion. People were screaming and there was the crunch of vehicles colliding. A billowing cloud of dust and smoke made its way around the corner and drifted into Albury. I had to fight the urge to go and help myself, and *I* knew it was a trick. Or I hoped it was, and not just a coincidence.

I edged Jack down the ramp towards the doors. The driver and both guards were Hrund, and the driver's mate seemed to be a Sithaari. They were all looking at each other, and up towards the apparent disaster. The doors to the underground parking bay were open, but not wide enough for me and Jack to squeeze past the guards. I muttered "go and help, go and help" to myself, as if I could will them to leave.

It was the driver who cracked first. He pushed his assistant in front of him and said, "Let's go," as he turned to hurry up the ramp. When he noticed the guards weren't following him, he turned back. "People could be hurt up there."

"Not our problem," said one guard, but I could see in his face that he wasn't happy. The other guard turned to look at him.

"I suppose, if one of us...?"

The first guard looked troubled, then gave a jerky nod. Three of them went up the ramp and headed off along the street while one stayed put. I stifled a groan. That wasn't the plan. And he was standing in exactly the wrong place, blocking our path through the gates. As if on cue, there was another mighty thump from the end of the street and the sound of falling debris. The remaining guard fidgeted, then ran up the ramp to see what was going on. I pulled hard on Jack's arm and we hurried forward.

We were in.

The underground space was astonishingly big; plenty of room for the delivery van to drive inside and turn around. To one side, there was a smarter area, with clean paint on the walls and a piece of red carpet on the floor in front of what looked like the grille for a lift. I wondered what sort of place this was that important people would want to come and go without being seen, then I turned my attention back to business. Awkwardly, with only one hand free, I put on my goggles and started tracking the Morph spoor. The agreement was that Jack would be our eyes in the mundane world, and he would keep a watch for me.

The Morphs had gone straight across the loading bay and through a double door on the opposite side. I cursed softly. Doors were a colossal risk. Even though neither I nor Jack would be seen, doors opening and closing on their own were a little conspicuous. At least these had windows in them, and I let Jack ease in front of me so he could look through. He pushed the door open after a hurried glance and we dashed inside.

The trail went straight along the corridor. I had hoped it would disappear off to a quieter part of the basement, but it seemed to do the opposite. There were no people near us, but the noise ahead was getting louder and more distinct, like the clatter of metal on metal with hissing and bubbling overtones. We came up to another set of doors, again with windows, and Jack swore when he looked through.

"What is it?" I whispered.

"A kitchen, and it's full of people."

Twenty-Seven

"What?" I rose onto tiptoe and tried to peer through the window, almost losing my grip on Jack's hand in the process. The trail went straight through and out a matching set of doors on the other side. "Can we make our way around the edges?"

"That's where the ovens and stuff are, and there are benches down the middle where food's being prepared."

That didn't fit with what I had seen. "But I saw the Morph trail, all the way across."

"Well, there is a gap between the tables, but it's only a couple of feet wide."

I thumped him with my free arm. "That's wide enough for us, idiot. So long as nobody else is using it."

There was a break in our conversation as Jack looked again, then he flattened back against the wall. "Someone's coming."

I tugged at his arm and hissed. "Double idiot. That's what we want. Which side of the door are they headed for?"

"Left. No, right," said Jack.

"One or the other," I complained, and at that moment, Jack pushed me to the right. A second later the left-hand door banged open and a Sithaari with an empty trolley pushed through and hurried down the corridor. The door was already closing as I pulled Jack through. I heard a thump from the door and felt Jack stumbled, so I guessed he clipped his heel or something. Nobody seemed to notice.

The kitchen was a mad clatter of activity, hot and steamy, with a deafening, perpetual cacophony of clattering and shouting from one end to the other. I couldn't breathe. Had I made a terrible mistake? Was there no way we could get across without someone noticing us? I worried about the billowing clouds of steam, too. Would the amulet still hide us, or would the mist eddy around us and show us up? I pushed the thoughts aside. We were where we were and I had to find a way out of, or through, the problem. I pushed Jack back against the wall next to the door while I pulled the goggles around my neck and looked across the kitchen.

"This is hopeless," Jack said in my ear. It was so noisy he was speaking in a normal voice. "We'll never get through. We have to find another way around."

I didn't answer, though the same thing occurred to me. What I didn't like about the idea was how long it might take us to find a different route, assuming one even existed. The amulet would only last so long. I watched the kitchen, the way it worked, the way the people moved, and tried to filter out Jack's fidgeting. A moment later, I tugged on his arm and he leant down to hear me.

"Look. There. See the pattern?"

Jack's eyes followed my pointing finger, and I prayed I wasn't inventing it, finding a pattern where none existed. Between the parallel rows of preparation tables, the traffic was much lighter. People doing the preparation worked on the outside. The inside space was only used by helpers bringing things to be worked on. They started at the same end as us and worked down the aisle before breaking away through a space in the middle. The process repeated in the second row. All we had to do was walk behind one of the assistants as they worked their way down the aisle.

"Might work," said Jack, "but if it doesn't, we're screwed."

I saw a female Grenlik carrying a half-dozen trays of vegetables head towards our end of the tables.

"Now," I said, and pulled Jack forward.

We stepped into the space between the two rows, just behind the Grenlik and keeping far enough back that she couldn't hear us or feel us disturb the air. We all moved halfway down the table before the Grenlik put a stack of trays on the left table, picked the stack up again minus the bottom tray and took two steps forward before repeating the process.

I felt something was about to go wrong, but I couldn't put my finger on what. Jack tapped my shoulder. I ignored him at first, still trying to figure out what it was that felt so wrong, but when he tapped again–this time more urgently–I looked over my shoulder and choked back a gasp. A second Grenlik, a male, was coming up behind them, servicing the other side of the tables. I had mistimed our entry.

The second Grenlik was moving more quickly. We were stuck in a sandwich. I moved us closer and closer to the girl Grenlik in front; so close that I was sure she must be able to feel our body heat. Jack hugged closer and closer to me as the male Grenlik worked his way down the table behind us. Trying to split my attention in both directions, I nearly stumbled into the female, then I saw the male behind us was down to his last tray.

We were all close to the end of the first row of tables now. The girl still had two more trays to drop. I looked back. The male dropped his last tray, too early, but then gave it a push and slid it towards the cook waiting for it. I held my breath. Would he try to squeeze past and bump into us? He looked, judging the space and how easy it would be to get through, then he turned and walked back up the row. I struggled not to let out a huge sigh of relief, but I was sure I felt Jack's hand tremble.

We repeated the process with the next table. Only one side was being used, and we could hurry along the gap when nobody was using it. The doors on this side were used more often, too, and we didn't have to wait long before we could follow someone through. As soon as we were past the doors, I slipped the goggles over my eyes and pinged the strap hard onto my ear with one-handed clumsiness. I didn't cry out, but my eyes misted up in a most unhelpful way.

I leaned against the wall for a moment. The absurdity of what we were doing made it feel like I was playing a computer game, and not a particularly good one. Some massive multi-user role-playing extravaganza with stunning graphics but no story. But this was no game, and that was what made my breath burn in my throat and my hands tingle. I closed my eyes for a moment, just to blink away the moisture, then looked over my shoulder to see if Jack was ready. I gave his hand a squeeze and got a jerky nod in reply. That made me feel guilty. He had to be scared, too, and he didn't have the comfort—if that was the right word—of being able to keep telling himself this was all for Evie. For a moment, I wondered why he had come along, but I pushed the thought away. We had a job to do.

The trail went along the corridor for a few yards, then turned off to the left. I set off, dragging Jack behind me. As soon as we turned away from the main corridor, everything got quieter. We turned another corner, and the trail took us up a narrow flight of stairs. The stairwell was more house-size than office-size. At the first landing, the trail turned off and doubled back more or less the way we had come.

The décor was a little better up here. Though the floor was still uncarpeted, it looked as though someone had polished it and there were fewer marks on the walls where trolleys had crashed into them. The lighting, oddly, was worse. Downstairs, there had been long strip lights everywhere, like fluorescent tubes, but still using magic. Here the lighting was from smaller fittings on the walls, which left pools of shadow every few yards.

The trail took another turn and as I followed it around the corner, I pulled up short and pushed Jack back.

"What is it?"

"There are two mountainous Hrund up there, guarding a door," I whispered.

"How far?"

"Not sure. Ten yards?"

"And that's where Jones is?"

"Don't know. I didn't check the trail. I just saw them and backed up."

Jack looked thoughtful for a moment. "Have another look and see if there's space to get past them."

I peered around the corner, afraid even though I knew they couldn't see me, then turned back to Jack. "I might squeeze past, but I'm not sure you could. It's narrow."

"And the trail?"

I shook my head. "I'm not sure."

"Huh?"

"The trail goes along the corridor, but I can't see if it goes into the room as well. The guards are in the way."

"So they might have brought her there, dropped her off, and carried on out the other way, or just gone through to somewhere else? Is that what you're saying?"

"Maybe." I knew I sounded defensive, but what did he expect? I could only see what I could see. "Should we use another distractor?"

"What are they?"

"One's screaming for help, and the other is a fake fire."

Jack frowned. "Either of them might bring people from all over the place. Opposite effect."

"So what do we do?"

Jack rubbed his free hand over his mouth and jaw. It looked like he had an idea, but he didn't like it much. "I have to draw them away," he said at last, and I knew I didn't like the idea either. "You can go on by yourself," Jack explained. "If she is in there, you can grab her and jump out. If she isn't—well, it's up to you if you follow the trail any further."

I didn't look at him. Couldn't. This wasn't how it was supposed to happen. "How will you get away from them?" There was no way of knowing what they would do to him, officially or otherwise, if they caught him, and I wasn't sure I could let that happen.

"I can mix in with a crowd, or jump out if it gets too tricky."

"Jumping out takes time. Concentration."

"I know. I'll make sure I stay well ahead of them. Just don't hang around when you find Jones. Shit, is she going to owe me some favours if we get her out of this." His face lost some of its seriousness and a playful smile crept over his lips and up to his eyes as he looked at her. "You, too."

My cheeks tingled, and I looked away. He didn't have to be doing this. Evie wasn't his friend, and I was pretty sure he wasn't convinced Evie was in here. Was he just doing this for me? My head spun at the thought, and at how worried I was that something might happen to him. Without thinking, I reached up with my free hand, put it behind his neck and pulled his face lower before I kissed him on the lips. "Be careful," I said, letting go of his neck before reaching into a pocket and pulling out a biro. Twisting their still clasped hands over, I started writing. "For when you get out. Right out, to the Over. Text me, or something, so I know."

Jack looked down at the digits written on the back of his hand. "I may never wash this again, you know," he said, and gave me an exaggerated wink. I resisted the temptation to use the pen to stab him in the arm and settled for giving him a scowl. "This is serious. Now, do you want a distractor?"

He seemed to think about it for a moment, then shook his head. "You might need them. As soon as you see me run down the corridor, step over to the other side. I don't want anyone crashing into you by accident. Ready?"

I wanted to say no, to find any reason that would postpone the moment when I would be left on my own and Jack would run off with two angry Hrund snapping at his heels. But I gave myself a stern talking to; I had already done things more dangerous and more stupid. Instead, I looked up at Jack and nodded.

"Remember, move over there," he pointed with his chin, then pulled his hand from mine and started around the corner. Then I watched in horror as Jack ran towards the guards.

Twenty-Eight

Halfway down the corridor, Jack seemed to notice the Hrund and slid to a stop. He hesitated, then made a terrible imitation of the black power salute from the eighties. "Capitalist thugs," he shouted. "Come on, come and get me, you gutless bastards. I'll never tell you where it is. Power to the revolution. You'll never find it before it goes off."

Both Hrund, who had been looking at Jack with idle curiosity and no small amount of contempt, suddenly paid an awful lot more attention. One stepped towards Jack with hands peacefully raised. "Hold on, sir. Are you telling me that—"

Jack was backing away. "You'll never find all of them. Not in time. Even if you catch me, I won't tell you."

He was almost back at the junction now. One Hrund was only a half-dozen steps from him, and the other was halfway between Jack and the door. He turned and ran. A split second later, so did the Hrund closest to him. The other walked up to the end of the narrow corridor and watched. He was so close I could touch him, but he showed no sign of joining the chase. The plan was falling apart.

I put my hand into my pocket. The main passageway went on for a dozen yards, then made a T-junction. I pulled both the remaining distractors out of my pocket and played a gamble.

Squeezing one to activate it, I touched it lightly to the back of the Hrund's tunic, where it stuck.

The countdown on this one was much shorter, only ten seconds. Tolks told me it would make someone think they could hear a cry for help in the distance, and it would keep leading them away from wherever it was activated. I heard the faint cries start, so quiet I was afraid the Hrund wouldn't hear them. His head turned this way and that, as if he was trying to judge where the noise was coming from, and his face got more and more concerned. He fidgeted, looking back towards the door, worried about deserting his post. I heard the cries for help get more insistent, and at the last minute realised I was standing right in the path the guard was going to take. I stepped to the side as he moved and was on my way down to the door as soon as I was sure the Hrund wasn't going to turn back.

It was a very ordinary door; simple, cheap and with plain handles. There was no keyhole, but someone had bodged a bolt onto the door at eye level. I grabbed it, pulled it back, and pushed the door open.

A wave of wrongness washed out over me just as I shifted my weight to move forward. I stopped myself an instant before I stepped into the room and peered inside. Evie was sitting on a chair in the middle of the room, looking at the door in confusion. I called out to her. Evie looked like she heard something but wasn't sure what, and I remembered the amulet dampened sound as well as sight. My hands were already touching the cord to lift it from my neck, but what if taking it off deactivated it? And would it switch back on? Dropping the cord, I wracked my brains for a way to get Evie close enough to touch, something she would trust. I pulled her old goggles over my head and threw them.

Evie's incredulous eyes tracked a pair of goggles that had appeared from empty air, headed towards her lap. They never got there. Evie snatched them out of the air, turning them over as she looked at them, and slowly recognised them. She stared at the doorway, frowning. Her eyes and mouth opened wide, and her hands came up, palms forward, as though pushing whoever was there away. "Stop. Don't come in. The room is a magic trap."

That was the wrongness I had felt, though 'how' was a question that would have to wait until later. Instead, I willed Evie to get off her backside and hurry over. She came to the door, but carefully, and she seemed to try to peer around the edges of the door before she was even in the doorway. As soon as her hand touched the doorframe, I placed my hand over it. Evie squealed and snatched her hand away, then started laughing.

"I knew it would be you," she said, holding her arms open. We hugged, and it surprised me how fiercely Evie held me. It also surprised me how well Evie looked. A little dishevelled, yes, but she looked clean and her clothes were exactly what I would have expected her to be wearing. Unless someone just laundered them for her, there was something else going on.

"I knew none of those idle, brain-dead, useless—" She took a breath. "I knew it would be you. Again." Evie relaxed the death-grip she had on me and held me out at arm's length. Then she noticed the amulet. "Is that Grenlik?"

"Is now the time to worry?" I replied. "We have to get you out of here." I changed things around until they were just holding hands and tugged.

"Wait," said Evie. "They may not even check." She let go of me, then pulled the door shut and pushed the bolt back. I let her grope around a couple of times before I caught her hand again. "Right. That might buy us some time. Now we can go. Let's get away from here before we try to jump out. Things still feel weird around here."

I led Evie back the way I'd come, but when we got to the stairwell, Evie dragged me to a halt. She was looking up the stairs, not down. "What are you doing? We have to get out."

"How long does this invisibility thing last?" Evie asked.

"No bloody idea, and I would rather be outside before we find out."

"I can't," said Evie.

There was a silence that lasted a heartbeat. "What?"

"I was investigating... something," Evie explained. "It's too complicated to go into now. They brought me here for a reason, but I think this is where they control whatever is going on. So where are we?"

"Stellar Cellar, and the place is crawling with people, so if we can just—"

"Natrak," Evie snapped her fingers and looked very pleased with herself. "I knew that scrawny vulture had something to do with this. We have to find out more. Which floor are we on?"

"One up from the basement. Look, do we have time?" I was getting annoyed that Evie didn't seem that impressed with the rescue, and was intent on getting herself, and me, captured again.

"Let's make time. I'll never get this chance again. They left me in that room for hours and I want some payback. We have to find his office, or close enough to it so I can jump back in here later."

"How can we find that? We have no idea of the layout of the place."

"We can make a good guess," said Evie, pulling me to go up the stairs. "Underland is a parasite. It steals from the Over, copies it, and hates change. Think of every nightclub you've seen in an old movie. What's the layout?"

I thought for a moment. "The boss' office looks out over the club from above."

Evie grinned, and we carried on up the stairs.

The stairway ended at a plain door. There was no window, and Evie opened it slowly. I flinched when she pulled the door wide open. "It's OK. Nobody there," she said over her shoulder as she dragged me through.

The corridor was plush, if tacky. Thick red carpet muffled our footsteps. The walls were covered with heavy fabric wallpaper in an even darker red, with a pattern embossed in black. Light came from ornate fittings on the walls, all dripping fake crystals like mini-chandeliers, or from equally dangly ceiling fittings surrounded by fancy plaster roses.

I was feeling like unappreciated baggage, or a convenient rack to hang the invisibility amulet on as Evie pulled me along the short corridor to the next junction. "Evie. This is crazy. Let's get out of here."

"Soon." She stopped and turned to face me. "Look, I know this seems nuts, but I'm onto something. Something truly important. If I just leave all I'll have is suspicions and questions. If I can get into his office, I can maybe get answers."

"Is that why you didn't jump out?"

"What? No. Don't be stupid. There's something weird about that room. You can't jump. I tried for hours."

She turned away, but I pulled her back. I realised that Evie thought they only locked her in the room for a few hours, full stop. Something had been playing with her sense of time. "And you want me to risk getting caught and stuck in here too? They have the police looking for you in the Over, Evie. You've been gone for nearly two weeks."

She looked shaken, but then her face went back to her 'resolved' look and I knew I'd lost. "We can sort all that out later. Look, if you want to bail, give me whatever kit you have and jump."

I nearly slapped her, and considered the option for several seconds before I dismissed it. "Not yet." I gave Evie's hand a harsh shake. "But don't think I won't, and don't think I'll wait around to swap amulets with you or give you your Kevlar back if I decide to go. This is really stupid." Evie nodded, then turned and led the way to the junction. I followed, not quite sure why, and trembling angrily.

The next corridor was as tastelessly decorated as the first. To the left, both sides of the corridor had doors every few feet. To the right, only one side was so heavily populated. "That way," said Evie, pointing right. "The rest are private rooms."

I wondered why a nightclub would need so many private rooms, and why Evie had put such a funny verbal twist on the word "private". Then my face burned like a bonfire and I tried not to think about it anymore.

Evie walked us to the closer of the two isolated doors and put her ear to it. She flinched away, turning back to me and putting a finger to her lips before moving on to the next door. I assumed she had heard something inside. I said nothing, even though I wanted to scream at Evie it was time to go. At the next door Evie listened, then listened some more before she tried the handle. The door clicked softly as it opened, and there was a faint hiss as it rubbed across the carpet. Once we were inside, Evie closed the door and twisted the lock before she let go of my hand.

The office was as tasteless as the corridor outside. The desk was oversized and inlaid with complicated veneers. Behind it was a huge, overstuffed leather chair on rollers. Two lesser chairs were in front of the desk, designed to show who the boss was, and there was a small table with four more chairs set off to one side. It was a room for doing business in, not entertaining. Two of the walls were little more than long windows, and were covered with slat blinds, all twisted closed.

Evie picked up one of the guest chairs and silently propped it under the handle of the connecting door before turning to the desk and rummaging through the papers. I hadn't a clue what I should look for, so I stayed out of the way and stayed invisible. It would be just our luck if I got too close, Evie bumped into me, and we knocked something over.

Instead, I walked to the window looking over the club and spread two of the blinds. It was an impressive view. The décor was still cheesy red and black, and from here I could see the long bar and most of the floor. It was still early, and very quiet. Where there was supposed to be a band, a pianist and a double bass filled in for mood music. A few of the booths had customers; some self-contained groups, others with one or two men being kept company by 'hostesses'.

Two of the hostesses were Hrund, and there were no Grenlix. The rest were tall and willowy with pumped chests. They looked like *femmes fatale* in tight sheath dresses and towering heels. Again, the dominant colour scheme was fire-engine red, with a preponderance of dark hair. They didn't look human, but I wasn't sure what race they came from. I did notice they all sat about as far away from each other as they could, and that there was a lot of mutual glowering going on.

I turned back to see what Evie was doing. She was still looking through the papers on the desk, and her expression suggested she hadn't found anything she hoped for. She let a last bundle of papers fall back more or less where she had taken them from, and she turned to look at the larger table. My shoulders slumped. How much longer? I turned away to look out the window again, but Evie chose that moment to let out a gasp. At the same time, the noise level from the room next door increased. It might have been laughter, and it didn't sound alarmed, but I looked back to the table and saw Evie was alert too. She was halfway through folding up a large sheet of paper.

After a moment, she carried on, stuffing the sheet into a pocket and reaching for another. With her other hand, she touched a finger to her eye and pointed to the window between the two rooms. I figured Evie wanted me to see what was going on next door.

I walked over to the wooden blind, the soft sound of folding paper behind me, and studied the problem. How could I move the blind? Nobody within would see me, but if anyone looked up, they would see the blinds twisted out of line. I edged back and forth, looking for a gap that would let me see what was going on. The gap was there, but it was small and I couldn't see much; the back of one person, who could have been an Angel, and the face of another. I frowned. Not Grenlik, Angel, Hrund or Sithaari, and as soon as I saw him, I felt a wrongness, like a soft echo of whatever lingered in Evie's prison.

Not sure why, I held my goggles up to my eyes, and almost dropped them when I looked through. The mysterious man glowed like a fresh Morph-trail. I knew I made no noise, and I knew I didn't touch the blind, but the instant I looked through the goggles, the strange being looked right at me. Directly. Eye to eye contact. An instant later, I felt a curious sensation, like a bubble around me popping, and I knew I had just become visible.

Twenty-Nine

"Evie," I called, trying to keep my voice low while still sounding urgent. The creature in the other room spoke to the Angel, though I couldn't make out what it said. "They know we're here." As the Angel rose from his seat, turning, the creature made eye contact with me again and she felt the same terrible wrongness that had saturated the room Evie had been in. "Get out," I yelled. "We can't jump."

The Angel was already at the connecting door, rattling the handle and pushing the door against the chair Evie had propped in front of it. I turned, heading for the other door, and saw Evie had frozen, stuffing yet another oversize sheet of paper into a pocket. "Out. Now."

I made one of the hardest decisions of my life and set off without Evie, even though I had invested all the time and effort to rescue her. If we were both caught, then there was only Jack. If he got caught too, nobody would ever come looking for any of us. I threw the office door open and went out into the corridor. Looking out from a different angle, I saw that the last door on the other side had a sign above it saying, "To the Club". My hand was already in my pocket, fingers activating the last distractor as I pulled it out and tossed it right in front of the door to the other room. Dense smoke billowed out, looking thick enough to walk on, and filled the width of the corridor in seconds. I took a last look over my shoulder. The smoke was almost to the office door, and Evie was just coming out. I gave her one more chance. "This way. Come on."

I didn't wait but pushed on through the door. The stairwell was better decorated, and obviously for customers and not staff, with carpeted stairs and moody lighting. I ran down the stairs and heard the door crash open again before I was halfway down the first flight. Alarm bells rang all over the club. As I reached the doors at the bottom, I heard Evie yell to me from above.

"Make for the front doors. Go with the punters."

Without answering, I pulled the door open and ran out onto the floor of the club.

For the first four or five steps, time seemed to slip into slow motion and detail flooded into me from all around. The pianist and the bass player were still performing but looking worried. The hostesses were ushering what customers there were towards a double door at the other end of the room and the barman was taking the cash tray out of his till. Hrund bouncers near the exit saw me but made no move to intercept me. The doors behind me crashed open again, presumably as Evie came through. I looked up at the gallery. The enraged face of an Angel looked down on me next to the calm and amused expression of the unknown monster. I stumbled to a stop, time returning to normal, and pulled my eyes away from the gallery just in time to see a Morph's tongue shooting towards my head.

I tried to duck and turn. Not my whole body; just my head. The Kevlar took the blow, spreading it out across the top half of my body, but it still knocked me from my feet and threw me backwards towards the bar. My head rang. Everything looked like it was in 3-D and I'd had forgotten my glasses. From my right came a dimly heard "Nooo" and the noise of furniture breaking. I sat up, shook my head, and looked around. A pair of hidden doors had opened in the wall below the gallery. Two

Morphs were sliming across the club, one towards me, the other towards Evie. She was throwing chairs at both of them, trying to distract them while I was on the ground. The bouncers were still out of the way at the main door and showed no interest in getting involved.

I fumbled at my leg for my PPG, but the holster clip was still in place. As I tugged at it to release it, a Morph got close enough to attack. Its mouth opened as the clip came off, but I knew I would never get the gun out or the safety off in time. I froze, waiting, watching, lifting my centre of balance forward onto the balls of my feet and tensing my muscles. Russian roulette. Penalty kick. At the slightest twitch of movement in the Morph's mouth I threw myself left.

The tongue/ fist/ nasty hard thing went by so close I was sure I felt a draft, but I didn't stop moving. I knew it took them several seconds to "reload" and I wanted to be out of range by then, or behind cover. I rolled to my feet and ran alongside the bar for a half dozen paces, then jumped onto it and rolled to the other side. As soon as I landed, I crouched and pulled the PPG out of its holster. My thumb flipped the safety off and I glanced down to check the charge. Full. I popped my head up over the bar as I took a quick sight on the Morph closest to me and fired. I didn't wait to see if I hit anything, just dropped below the bar again and crawled.

There was a crash from somewhere in front of me, and my first thought was that Evie was hit. When I got to the other end of the bar, I poked my head out until I could see what was going on. Both Morphs were now attacking Evie, and she was being herded into a corner. Perfect. I moved a little farther out so that I could get a clear shot and took my time to aim.

I fired twice at the Morph closest to Evie then, while the shots were still in the air, I shifted my aim and fired two more shots into the second. On the fourth shot, the gun made a strange cough, and the last cloud didn't look right, but it didn't matter. Both Morphs exploded into puddles of slippery goo. Evie picked her way through the mess and ran to take cover with me. "Let's get out of here."

I nodded and wrapped myself in the intention of leaving, but something still interfered with my jump. From the anger and confusion on her face, Evie was also having a problem. She held out her hand. "Let me see that damned gun."

I handed it over. Evie turned it on its side. I gasped and Evie looked somehow defeated. The charge crystal showed the gun was empty, which was impossible. The gun was supposed to hold charge for six shots and, even for this earlier, less efficient model, it should have been able to recharge enough for two more shots by now.

"What do we do?" I asked.

Evie looked thoughtful for a moment. "If we only knew what was stopping us jumping."

I pointed to the observation window. "Up there. With the Angel. I don't know what he, it, is, but I think he's causing it."

"Then let's get as far away from him as we can. Crawl down to the other end of the bar. We can rush the bouncers and get out with the crowd."

I did as Evie suggested. I didn't think the crowd was big enough to hide in, but it was the best idea we had. When I got to the other end, I could see people, hostesses, and no bouncers. I stood up, ready to hurry over to the small crowd still pushing to get through the doors and away from the violence.

I had only taken two steps when a Hrund bouncer stepped out from behind one of the main doors, twenty feet in front of me. He had a hand-bow in his right hand and was holding his left hand out, palm forward. "Stop right there. Put your weapon on the ground and kick it away."

I looked down and realised that I had automatically lined the PPG up with the bouncer's chest. Even if there had been enough charge in it to fire, I doubted it could hurt him. Then I wondered if he knew that. Hand-bows, which were basically miniature crossbows, were single shot. The string had to be pulled back and a new quarrel fitted each time they were fired. Admittedly, his looked odd, but maybe that was because it was unlicensed and illegal. My weapons training told me a hand-bow couldn't penetrate a Kevlar.

"No, drop yours, or I'll fire," I said, trying to sound like I meant it. The Hrund's eyes narrowed, and I tried to decide if he was doubting me or the weapon. Or both. If she could get him to shoot at her, then his weapon would be useless and they could get past him and get out. I twitched my PPG up, as if firing it. The Hrund fired too.

The little quarrel slammed into my right shoulder, knocking me backward a half-step. My arm swung outwards, throwing the useless PPG across the club, and I twisted my balance back again, ready to run forward.

The second quarrel hit my other shoulder, and I staggered back another step, pushing Evie back and sideways. What other quarrel? There shouldn't have been another. As I looked back at the bouncer, I saw another bolt already loaded in the hand-bow. That was impossible. Did he have more than one? There was another dull twang, and the bolt took me in the centre of my chest.

I fell backward, Evie's Kevlar burned my skin, and I dragged glasses and bottles from the back of the bar. I looked up at the Hrund. He had stepped closer, was looming over me. He had a savage grin, a wide, wild look in his eyes, and I knew he was going to fire again. How was he reloading so fast? The hand-bow played another deep note, and I cried out. The amulet stung my skin, and the bolt thumped into my shoulder; not hard enough to cut through my heavy coat, but hard enough I knew I would have a huge bruise to explain.

"Stop," Evie screamed, close by me. "Can't you see her Kevlar is down? We surrender."

But the bouncer had taken another step closer. His eyes still shone with ugly delight in what he was doing and his hand came up to point the weapon at my head. His finger tightened on the trigger and with a last shriek of "No!" Evie was in the air and between the bouncer and me.

The thrum of the hand-bow was followed by a sickening, meaty *thwock*, Evie seemed to fall faster towards me, a look of surprise on her face. She landed hard and my arms instinctively folded around her. As the bouncer raised his weapon again, I demanded to be somewhere else. I didn't care where, and I didn't care when, but I reached for that place I used when I needed to jump, fighting past whatever was trying to stand in my way, grabbed hold of the Over and *pulled*.

Thirty

As soon as we arrived wherever I had taken us, my mobile started howling for attention. Evie tried to lift herself off me but cried out and fell back.

"Can you hold yourself up on your other arm?" I gasped. Evie's weight robbed me of breath. "Maybe I can slide out and help you up."

She didn't say anything, but I saw muscles ripple along her jaw. A moment later, the weight lifted off my chest. I slid sideways and rolled to my knees, turning to help take Evie's weight. As we struggled to our feet, Evie started to chuckle, balancing uncontrollable humour against the pain of the bolt sticking out of her right shoulder.

"Can't jump, eh?" she said, her voice thin.

I looked up, frowned, and shook my head in disbelief. Across the road was the entrance to Chaine Farm Hospital A&E department. The last time I had been here was five years ago, when I cracked a bone in my wrist. I had jumped us to within thirty feet of the doors.

As we stumbled across the road to the emergency room, I realised we still had a problem. "Why are we here?"

Evie picked up on the problem straight away. "Oh rats. We don't have any time and I can't think straight. You'll have to come up with something."

"Me? Again? That's not fair."

Evie mixed laughing and groaning in equal measure as we crossed the road, and I had to join in. There was a weird, twisted irony to it. "You can't remember a thing," I said after a moment. "Me and my boyfriend found you wandering at the side of the road. He couldn't wait."

"You don't have a boyfriend," Evie argued. We had reached the other side of the road and she was working her good hand around her coat, picking out folded sheets of paper and Underland contraband. I tried to hide them as fast as she handed them to me.

"I can get one," I said.

"In five minutes?" Evie gave me a look that questioned my sanity.

"Hope so."

Evie chuckled again, but this time her knees seemed to lose interest in keeping her upright and I had to grab her arm and help steady her. A passing nurse noticed us, saw the blood running from Evie's back, and rushed over. Then the NHS took over and whisked Evie away in a wheelchair.

I was shown to a waiting room and an eagle-eyed nurse outside watched to make sure I didn't break out and try to make a run for it before the police arrived. She scowled at me when I fiddled with my phone, but I was too tired to care. There were ten missed calls and twelve texts, and it was only then that I realised I hadn't snapped back. The same time I spent in Underland had passed in the Over, and it was now very late in the evening. I had mysteriously disappeared from home before dinner. That was the first thing to sort out. I dialled home, and after "Hello, mum," spent the better part of five minutes listening to my mother having minor hysterics before I could get a word though in any direction, let alone sideways.

"Mum, listen. I need you to come and pick me up."

"Where are you? What's happened? I'm calling the poli—"

"Mum, I don't have much battery left. Can you come and get me? I'm at the Chaine Farm A&E—"

"Ohmygod, ohmygod, ohmygod, whatever has happened, are you hurt ohmyg—"

"I'm fine. Totally. Look, can you just come get me and I'll explain everything when you get here?"

I pushed the button to disconnect the call, prayed that my father would be driving, and started looking through my texts. The first six were from Mum or Dad, as were the last five. The seventh made me break out in a huge smile of relief. I opened the message from the unknown number.

The entry simply said "Safe", but I knew who it was from. I saved the number against the name "Jack" and sent a text back.

"You are now officially my boyfriend." I added a quick outline of the story I was going to use, then deleted both the inbound and outbound texts.

My parents turned up moments before the police, who had been called by the hospital. As soon as they realised that Evie was the missing girl, many questions were asked. I stuck to my simple lie; Me and a boyfriend my parents didn't know about—because I didn't think they would approve of him—had been driving around and had seen a girl stumbling down the street. We had slowed, saw she was hurt, stopped and offered to take her to the hospital, which was nearby. The girl had seemed confused and didn't know her name or where she was. My boyfriend couldn't spend hours hanging around the hospital, so he had dropped them at the A&E and gone home while I helped the girl inside.

Nobody was happy with the story, but there was nothing to disprove it, and my dad eventually convinced the police to let us go home. I sat in the back seat, eyes heavy. Mum was babbling, Dad was concentrating on the road, and the slightly over-warm air soothed my exhausted body. I twisted around until I was lying on my side, knees bent, arms folded in front of me. I ached. I was going to have a monster bruise on my shoulder, and I was deeply weary. As I watched the streetlights flash overhead, I pushed aside all the thoughts and questions that still rattled around my head. I could deal with them another day. For now, I had been right. I warned them someone had captured Evie and had even rescued her. They would have to reinstate me. As my eyelids became too heavy to hold up, I realised how important that was to me.

How much I wanted to be Warrior Stone.

Thirty-One

Being grounded isn't so much of a problem when you can jump into another world from your bedroom. I gave myself a couple of days, then did just that—but only to speak to HR. I wasn't ready to go back on duty, and I certainly wasn't ready to confront Aslnaff. I needed Evie for that.

It took Evie a week before she felt ready to return to Underland. We timed it so Aslnaff would be having his weekly meeting with the sub-committee of the Grand Council that oversaw the SFU. We breezed past the secretary, who tried to stop us but wasn't fast enough. I threw the doors open, and Evie marched in first.

"What is the meaning of this?" Aslnaff screamed. "Out, or I'll have—"

"Our profound apologies, Councillors," said Evie. "This will take just a moment of your time. Despite my fellow Warrior—"

"She has been demoted, and now will be dismissed—"

"A moment, supervisor," said one of the Hrund, raising his hand. "I would know what would cause two humans to so interrupt this meeting. Any second?"

A Grenlik also raised his hand, and the Hrund nodded.

"I am Warrior Jones," said Evie. "Some of you may have heard of me." There were a couple of nods, and at least as many frowns, and one chuckle. "My fellow Warrior realised several weeks ago that I was missing. The Unit dismissed her concerns, suggesting I had gone missing in our own world or simply aged out, despite my fellow Warrior presenting compelling evidence to the contrary."

"And the point of this interruption?" The Hrund asked.

"Just this. I was in Underland, being held against my will for several weeks. When my fellow rescued me, we were assaulted with illegal repeating hand bows, and almost lost our lives. I make no accusations at this time but would ask the sub-committee to consider two requests. The first is that my fellow is re-instated to the rank of Warrior. Her probationary period has expired, and she has shown she is more than competent for the position."

Which surprised the heck out of me. We hadn't discussed this, but it was exactly the sort of thing she would do. I kept my face professional and bland. As much as I could, anyway.

"And the second request?"

"If the sub-committee sees fit, a full investigation into the events around my abduction and illegal restraint."

The Hrund looked thoughtful, then shared a look with the Grenlik who has seconded his motion. I didn't see a nod, or anything like that, but some kind of communication passed between them.

"Thank you for bringing these issues to our attention, Warriors. There will be no decisions at this time, but we will advise you of any that are made. Now, if we could return to our business at hand?"

I swear there was a faint smile on the Hrund's face. Evie and I both bowed deeply to the room and backed out, then closed the door. I let out a breath I didn't know I had been holding, and we shared a look that threatened to become a laugh. Until I heard a sharp tap-tap-tap behind us. I turned, and Aslnaff's secretary was tapping her pen against a nail on her other hand.

"You two will take a step too far one day, and there may be nobody there to catch you next time. Do *not* do that again, or I shall mess up your paperwork so badly it will take you a year to sort it out."

With a flick of her finger's, she dismissed us, and we hurried from the room after throwing her contrite bows. There were a few things to sort out with HR, and Evie insisted on checking that stores had replaced everything in her locker, then we headed for Cotton Street.

Tolks' shop looked different. I'd only been there a couple of weeks ago, but it looked like it had been closed for a year or more. Paint was peeling off the door, and the window was painted over, on the inside, by that white stuff shopfitters use when they don't want you looking inside. We rapped on the door.

"Closed!"

Evie and I shared a smile, then both of us pummelled on the door at the same time. It flew open and Tolks scowled at us.

"Impudent humans. Inside, before you embarrass me further."

Evie strolled straight into the workshop, but I waited and walked with Tolks. It was his place, after all. Seemed the polite thing to do. When we were all in the workshop, Tolks set about making coffee and said very little until it was done. Though it was uncomfortably hot against my fingers, I held the cup up to my nose to enjoy the smell while it cooled enough to drink.

"So what foolishness did you immerse yourself in this time?" Tolks snapped at Evie. He sounded so angry it surprised me, and even made Evie's eyes widen.

"I was following a hunch."

"A hunch? About what?"

"Morph's screw with the local magical field, right?"

Tolks nodded and sipped. "This is well known."

"But why? And do they only mess with it while they are here, or somehow before? And why do they run once they emerge? Wy don't they just translate right up to our world as soon as they arrive here?"

Tolks looked like he was going to say something, but the thought collapsed on him.

"So I started checking it out. If we could tie down any of those, it would make stopping them easier. Imagine if we could predict where they were more likely to break through based on that day's field density report, either because they were picking a weak area to come through because it made it easier, or because they weakened the field in advance?"

Tolks nodded. "Noble objectives. Did you not consider that others may have done such work before you? We have lived in this world considerably longer than you."

Evie was pulling a sour face. "You'd think, wouldn't you. Ever heard of anything like it?"

"Well..."

"I checked the public library, the SFU archive, I even asked the Grenlik Academy, and they made the same noise you did. The Angels wouldn't help me, the Hrund had no information, and the Heavy Engineering department wouldn't even take my call."

I'd never heard of any Heavy Engineering department, and I was just about to ask about them when Tolks spoke ahead of me.

"So, typical Jones, you thought you would go and do it yourself?"

"Isn't that what they say to do if you want a job done right?"

Tolks nodded again, though reluctantly. "And has your research brought any conclusions?"

Evie's face soured. "Not yet. But there's something there. I just haven't dug deep enough yet."

"What about that hole?" I asked.

Evie snapped her fingers and pointed at me. "Exactly. Under that building there's a dent in the local field like a black hole, and for a block around it everything is unstable."

I hadn't a thing to say. This was all so far over my head clouds could have passed under it. Tolks was thinking, hard, staring into his coffee cup like he was trying to avoid looking at either of us. Evie watched him like a dog watching someone holding a ball, full of anticipation and eagerness. When Tolks looked up, I could tell right away she was in for a disappointment.

"My suggestion is you should abandon this investigation."

"What?"

"For your own good."

"But this is important."

Tolks nodded. "Perhaps, perhaps. But if there is some malign force at work here, you are putting yourself in great danger. Think. They have already captured and imprisoned you, and who knows what their plans for you might have been."

Evie, angry as I'd ever seen her, drew breath to argue. Tolks raised a finger, and much to my amazement, Evie held her tongue.

"Second, you are investigating something you do not possess the qualifications to fully understand. This is a magical issue. Humans can not directly interact with magic. Whilst the tool you have is an aid to analysis, it is not ideally suited to wide area data gathering, and its result must be balanced against other factors which you would not be able to appreciate."

"So I'm too stupid? Some silly little monkey playing with something bright and shiny she picked out of the gutter?" Evie put her cup down, hard, but not enough to hurt it, and slid off her stool. "I thought you understood me better than that."

Tolks raised his hands and called "Jones, wait," but Evie stormed out of the workshop and, a moment later, I heard the shop door slam shut.

Tolks' shoulders slumped and he sighed. "Wilful child. She means well, but she drives herself so hard. One day, she will involve herself in something from which she cannot escape." He looked up at me. "Or from which her friends cannot rescue her."

And now I felt awkward, like someone hanging on at the end of a thing when everybody important had already left. I started coming up with an excuse for my own exit, but Tolks pulled his stool closer to mine and climbed onto it.

"There is nothing else we can do to help Warrior Jones, at least for now. Her anger must run its course. But now, let us turn our attention to you."

"Me?" The word came out in a squeak.

He smiled. "Of course. You asked a favour, and stated you were willing to pay the price. Payment is now due."

A ball of ice formed in my gut. I'd said something like that, but now, alone with this Grenlik I had only met three or four times, I was suddenly aware of how absurdly stupid I'd been. He was far enough away. I could jump off my stool and get out of the workshop, then far enough across the shop so I could jump out before he could do anything to me.

But he was still sitting there, looking at me, and for all the world it looked like he knew what I was thinking, and was waiting to see if I would run. Was he *judging* me?

Everybody said you can't trust a Grenlik, but every single one I'd met had helped me when I asked, from Krossett in Stores, through to the doorman at the hive. Sharing names was a mark of respect, a sign that they thought I was a worthy person. Maybe I should have thought more about how I was returning the respect. I hadn't, until now, properly understood. What had

Tolks ever done to me that should make me wary of him now, when I hadn't even heard what he wanted from me yet?

"And how can I settle the debt?" I said, struggling a little to keep my voice even.

"Take this," he said, passing me a metal rod from the worktop. It was about a foot long and had a ball on the end. "Hold it towards me and do not let go. There may be some discomfort."

Seemed safe enough. It was quite heavy, so I took it in both hands. Tolks went to his own bench and came back with a box that looked like a very modern meter, except it also had a metal ball. He fiddled with the settings and held his meter out until it almost touched my bar. A purple cloud, almost the same colour as the discharge of a PPG, formed around the two balls. A moment later, my fingers started to tickle, then pins and needles washed over both hands. I told Tolks, and he nodded.

Then there was a second test, with a large crystal. That made a fat spark and hurt like the worst static bolt ever. I complained.

"My apologies. One more."

This time it was a wooden stick, at the end of which was a four-point star made of windings like my Kevlar, with a glowing gemstone in the middle. This made my hands feel warm, then there was another bright spark and a loud snap.

"Tolks, I'm feeling tired now. Do we have to finish this now?"

"We are done," he said, taking the metal stick away from me and putting everything back on his own bench.

"And?" I couldn't decipher his expression. He looked pleased, but I think there was surprise, too. Or perhaps not surprise. Something deeper, like wonder. He came to sit next to me again.

"Of all the races in Underland, only two can use magic."

"Two? I thought it was just Grenlix."

"There is another. We do not need to discuss them now. But I'm sure you have been told Humans cannot?"

"Sometime. Not sure when."

"Because this is not your world, or so we believe."

"Tolks, is there a point to this? I am really tired and—"

"I believe you are, somehow, an exception. You sensed the magical field around Jones when she was captured, and you felt when the invisibility charm was disabled. You pushed your way through an interdiction and forced a jump you should not been capable of. Yes, I am certain."

He leaned forward and gimlet eyes bored into mine.

"You can use magic, Miss Stone, and I can teach you how."

— o —

If you enjoyed this book, a little review goes a long way. Visit www.robinhartfantasyauthor.com for some nice easy links to leave reviews, or for more information on the books.

Thank you

Robin

Printed in Poland
by Amazon Fulfillment
Poland Sp. z o.o., Wrocław